Raves For the Work of DONALD HAMILTON!

"Hamilton is a pure storyteller of the first rank... masterly, dark, and constantly surprising."
—*Ed Gorman*

"His stories are as compelling and probably as close to the sordid truth of espionage as any now being told."
—*The New York Times*

"His capacity to divert is spectacular."
—*New York Herald Tribune*

"Fast, tightly written, brutal, and very good."
—*Milwaukee Journal*

"A yarn that keeps moving at an irresistible pace... written in a style that builds suspense upon suspense. This man is good!"
—*Edward S. Aarons*

"If you have half a dozen thrillers at hand and one is by Donald Hamilton, you can either grab it at once or save it for dessert."
—*New York Herald Tribune*

"Never fails to pull off a first-rate adventure."
—*The Hartford Courant*

"Take me with you, David," she said. "We'll be Mr. and Mrs. Wilson, hear? We'll go—somewhere. Nobody will know."

He said, "Elizabeth—"

"Think it over. There's also the money."

Young said, "I wouldn't touch a cent of that bastard's—"

Elizabeth smiled. "You've taken his name and his home, you've been eating his food; you've kissed his wife. Why get high-minded about the money?"

Young looked at her; and she waited. The light from the open window made her look young and expectant and quite lovely. It occurred to him, rather shockingly, that he now knew this girl better than he knew any other person in the world.

You could put it nicely, he thought, and say that they seemed to get along well together because they suited each other; or you could make it ugly and say that they damn well had better get along because they knew too much about each other not to. Either way, they got along, and he knew suddenly that they always would, because neither of them would ever expect too much of the other. They would always make allowances. Both of them knew that there was not a great deal to expect.

He said, looking up at her, "You don't know what I look like. You've never seen my face."

"I'll like it," she said. "If I don't, I can always—close my eyes, like this." Smiling, she bent down and kissed him full on the mouth.

He looked at the girl standing above him, and thought, Why not?

"Hell," he said, "It's a deal..."

OTHER HARD CASE CRIME BOOKS
YOU WILL ENJOY:

Night WALKER

by **Donald Hamilton**

A HARD CASE CRIME BOOK
(HCC-016)
January 2006

Published by

Dorchester Publishing Co., Inc.
200 Madison Avenue
New York, NY 10016

in collaboration with Winterfall LLC

ISBN 0-8439-5586-4

Printed in the United States of America

Visit us on the web at www.HardCaseCrime.com

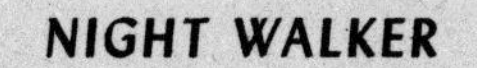

NIGHT WALKER

Chapter One

He ran after the twin taillights as a car finally swerved to the side of the highway in response to his thumb signal. The driver pushed the door open for him, and sent the big coupé away again with a rush the moment he was inside. David Young found space for his bag between his feet and settled back against the cushions to watch the highway come reeling into the headlights with swiftly increasing speed. He did not, these days, like fast driving, and as the big car lunged into a curve he could not help bracing himself in the seat, while through his mind flashed again, unwanted, memory of disaster that had nothing to do with automobiles.

The driver beside him spoke. "Kind of late at night to be hitchhiking, Lieutenant."

"I'm supposed to report at Norfolk in the morning," Young said. "Thanks for stopping. That gravel shoulder gets hard on the feet."

"Forget it," the man said. "Nobody minds helping out a guy who looks like he's willing to try hoofing it if he has to. It's these damn helpless jerks with two suitcases and a portable radio—" He spat out the open window beside him—a dim, husky figure in a light hat and topcoat. There was not enough illumination for Young to try to guess his age; but in spite of his rough way of speaking he had a well-to-do look about him that matched the car he was driving. Young looked away, remembering that even when you were in uniform people were always a little uneasy about picking you up along the road, particularly at night; there was no point in worrying his benefactor by seeming in a hurry to look him over. The man spoke again: "Been on leave, Lieutenant?"

"No." Young could not help making the answer short. "Reporting for duty."

"Called back, huh?"

"That's right."

"Tough," the man said. He took his eyes from the road briefly and seemed to study Young's appearance, his eyes finally reading the ribbons on the Lieutenant's uniform blouse; then he checked the car expertly as it began to stray. "Looks like you saw some action in the last one, Lieutenant. Pacific theater, eh? Wounded, too." He glanced back at the ribbons. One caught his eye and he whistled softly as he returned his attention to the road. "Got one of the big ones, eh? Don't see too many of those around." He drove for a while in silence, perhaps waiting for Young to respond to this. When his passenger did not speak, the man went on: "You'd think this time they'd pick on the boys who sat the last one out, like yours truly. I suppose you had yourself all fixed up with a job and family, too, like a lot of the other guys they're pulling back in."

Young shook his head. "No. I was still going to school under the G.I. bill, as a matter of fact. Graduate work in engineering. It looks as if I'll be nursing a long gray beard when I finally get that degree. But no family, thank God."

"Just the same, it's tough," the man said. He added slyly, "You'd think that, yanking you back that way, the Navy would at least advance you enough for train fare."

Young flushed slightly. "They did," he said. "Uniforms and transportation both. Only, well, I got a little high the other night—"

The driver chuckled. "I thought you looked kind of like the tail of a rough weekend. Celebrating, eh?"

"You might call it that," Young said.

He was glad when the man beside him did not ask for details; he did not like to think of how drunk he had been.

He leaned back against the seat wearily, removing his cap so that he could lie back comfortably. Presently he found himself looking at the cap in his hands; it had a raw and new look that did not appeal to him. The gold lace was very bright; the device shone silvery against its dark background. It might, he reflected distastefully, have been the cap of a baby ensign fresh from the trade school on the Severn that was located not so far from here. He could remember a really well-broken-in cap that he had lost on an occasion he preferred not to think about; and one not quite so salty-looking, but still quite presentably dilapidated, that he had given away. He had got rid of everything when they released him to inactive duty in 1946; he'd had his war, he remembered thinking, somebody else could take the next one. He had picked a school inland where water was something you used for washing, and for drinking if you couldn't do better. He had not stepped aboard as much as a rowboat in seven years.

The headlights picked out the signs announcing the approach of *Rogerstown, Maryland, Population 7000, Speed Limit 25, Enforced.* The marked slowing of the car as they approached the darkened business area made Young glance at the driver, who had not impressed him as a person who took speed limits seriously.

"I turn off up ahead, Lieutenant," the man said. "Sorry I can't take you any farther. Hope you make out all right."

Young concealed his disappointment. "Sure," he said. "Thanks."

He watched the intersection approach, and lifted

his bag from between his feet, preparing to get out of the car when it should stop. Then the man glanced at him, seemed to hesitate nervously, and motioned to him to sit still, pressing down the gas pedal so that the coupé shot ahead again. The signposts and the stop light—dark so late at night—flashed past; then the town also was behind them. The driver laughed at Young's questioning frown.

"Hell, I'll run you into Washington, Lieutenant. You'll grow roots like a tree trying to catch a ride out here in the middle of the night." He reached into his hip pocket and brought out a wallet, selected a bill from the proper compartment, one-handed, and held it out to Young. When Young hesitated, he said with a show of irritation, "Ah, take it! I'll drop you at the bus station and this'll get you to Norfolk. You can send it back when you get paid."

Young frowned, not entirely pleased by the other's generosity. "Look, you don't have to—"

"Skip it, skip it," the driver said. "Hell, it's the least I can do, isn't it?"

Young said, "Well, it's damn white of you, but—"

The man dropped the ten-dollar bill into his lap. "Hell, it's nothing, Lieutenant. I'll get my money back, won't I? And you're not taking me a damn bit out of my way. I was heading for Washington, anyway. I was just going to stop off to see my wife on my way down from New York; she's staying at our place over on the Bay. But it's a forty-mile drive and the roads aren't too good; and she'd a damn sight rather have me in the daytime, anyway. We haven't been getting along lately, I can make it on my way back north."

Young picked up the money reluctantly; it made him feel like a drunken bum accepting a handout. His pride wanted him to refuse the loan, but common sense told him to take it. Reporting for duty late would not improve his situation any, and there was no point in hurting the feelings of a man who was trying to do him a favor.

"Well, if you're sure—"

"I said, skip it."

"If you'll give me your name and address—"

"You can send it to Bayport; my wife will see it gets to me. Lawrence Wilson, Bayport, Maryland." Wilson held out his hand. "My friends call me Larry."

"Dave," Young said, taking the hand. "Dave Young."

"Okay, Dave," Wilson said. He gave his passenger's uniform another glance before returning his attention to the road. "I used to be in the Navy myself, in a way," he said presently. "Only quit last year." Then he laughed sharply. "Quit, hell! Who am I trying to kid, anyway? You're looking at a dirty red subversive, Dave."

Startled, Young turned to look at the man beside him, thinking that some kind of a joke was intended.

Wilson's expression was obscured by the shadow of his hat brim; but it was clear that he was not smiling.

"But what—"

"That," said Wilson, "is what I've been trying to find out for a year now. What?"

"You mean they didn't tell you—"

"Brother, you don't know the setup. Nobody has to tell you anything, see. It's that kind of a deal. They get 'information' that you're a risk to departmental 'security.' You get a couple of hearings, but what the hell good does that do? You don't know what you're fighting against. All you can do is tell them what a swell guy you are and how much you love the United States of America. They've heard that routine before. So you go, and your friends hear about it and start acting funny, too! Everybody looking at you like they expected you to pull a hammer and sickle out of your pants pocket....Nuts!" Wilson said bitterly. "I tell you, Dave, when it happens to you, you learn a lot of things about your friends and family you didn't know before. Even the ones who don't believe it about you stay away because they're scared to be seen with you any longer." The man glanced at Young. "Maybe *you* want to give me back that ten-spot and start walking, now!"

Young shifted uncomfortably in the darkness, because the accusation was not far from the truth. His first instinct had been to get out of this. It was, after all, none of his problem; and he did not want to get mixed up in it, particularly in uniform. But now, directly challenged, he had to shake his head. Still it seemed strange that Wilson should tell so much to a complete stranger. It was almost as though the man wanted to be sure Young would remember him.

"You don't know what it's like," Wilson said presently. "Even a leper gets sympathy, but not a guy in my spot. Except from the radicals and crackpots who figure that because the government fired me I must be one of the boys. You'd be surprised how easy—" He checked himself abruptly.

The big coupé ran on through the night at high speed. Young tried to relax, but the speed made him uneasy, and he did not like the feeling of having brushed against the edge of a dark world of which he had no knowledge or understanding. He warned himself against the instinctive sympathy he felt for Wilson's predicament; after all, he had nothing but Wilson's own unsupported word for his innocence, and it was none of his business, anyway. He had problems enough of his own.

"Dave," the man beside him said.

"Yes?"

"I bet you think I'm kind of a damn fool, spilling all this crap to a guy I never saw before. Well, to hell with it. You don't know if I'm telling the truth and there's no way I can prove it, yet. One day there are going to be some people with red faces around

Bayport, and I mean red, get it? But right now let's skip it. What about you? You're not regular Navy, are you; you haven't got the ring..."

They talked for a while. Young gave the name of the university to which he had been going; in answer to the other's questioning—Wilson was the kind of a man to whom the most personal inquiries seemed to come quite naturally—he said that his parents were dead and that he was not only not married, he had no particular girl in mind for the honor. He said that he had originally joined the Navy because he had done some sailing as a kid and liked boats. Wilson brightened at this information.

"Say, if you like boats, maybe you'd like to see a picture of one I designed for a friend of mine. That's my field, you know, ship design. This one's a thirty-foot sloop, a little smaller than the stuff the Navy had me on...."

Driving one-handed, he produced his wallet again, and tried to find something among the licenses and identification cards shielded in clear plastic and hinged to form a sort of book. Young waited. The glow from the luminous dashboard gave Wilson very little light to work by; he had to look up quickly to pull the car back as it ran out onto the shoulder of the highway. In the dim light it was hard to tell, but Young was almost sure Wilson's hand was shaking as he handed over the wallet.

"You find it; it's in there somewhere. There's a map light in the glove compartment, if it feels like working."

Young opened the compartment and leaned forward to hold the wallet under the light that came on automatically. Leafing through the cards, he came on a snapshot of a white sailboat made fast to a dock. A girl was standing in the cockpit, facing the camera self-consciously, sunburned and in bathing costume. She was quite small, and had an intriguing, innocent, tomboyish look about her.

"That's it." Wilson let the car's momentum carry it along with decreasing speed as he looked over Young's shoulder.

"Nice-looking craft," Young said. "Is that your wife?"

"Elizabeth?" Wilson laughed sharply. "Hell, no. Just try to get her on a boat! No, that's Bunny; we've sailed together since we were kids. She's the only one who—stuck by me after that Washington business broke. Got her folks to give her a boat for Christmas and then asked me to design it for her, to give me something to do except brood, I guess. I knew she was doing me a favor, but I wasn't going to turn it down. We worked on it together, as a matter of fact; she told me what she wanted in the way of racing gadgets and general layout and I did the calculating and the drawing up of the lines....She's a pretty slick little bucket, eh? I wish I had a shot that showed you the lines, but you can make out the rig, all right. It takes three or four to race her right; but even a girl can handle her easy, for cruising." Wilson's voice was insistent and his words seemed to be coming faster now. "The binnacle is set into the cockpit floor where it's out of the way. We've got good big winches for the jib sheets..."

As Young leaned forward to study the details, there was a quick movement beside him; then something hit him across the head harder than he had ever been struck before. He tried to struggle upright, dazed and bewildered; but the man beside him, still talking rapidly as if to deceive some unseen observer—perhaps his own conscience—struck a second and a third time, driving his passenger down into black unconsciousness.

Chapter Two

It was the same old nightmare. Young recognized it at once although a long time had passed since the last one; so long that he had congratulated himself on having the thing licked. But here it was again, and he lay watching it unfold in his mind, knowing exactly what was coming, knowing that it was a nightmare, but feeling himself, as always, helplessly drawn into it and swept away by it.

It took the same course as always. They were blacked out and making standard speed through a nearly calm sea when the torpedo hit forward. The one amidships followed almost immediately. He was aware, as he listened for orders and shouted some of his own—his voice cracking as he tried to make it carry over the noise—of the ship losing way and taking a sharp list to port. He was out on the flight-deck now and a roar and a hot breath of flame told him that the high-octane gas for the planes was going up. It was no longer dark. A squawking voice was repeating the order to abandon ship. There was fire everywhere and she was being shaken by a series of jolts and jars from below. He heard the screaming nearby, saw where it came from, wrapped something about his head, and started for it, wondering how much time he had. Everything seemed to be in slow motion; yet time seemed to be moving very fast. He was working furiously, less conscious of what he was doing than of the time rushing past him. *Now* it comes, he thought, *now,* and *now.* But it did not come, and then he was finished and over the side, and there was fuel oil on the water and the ship's flaming bulk continued to drift down on him no matter how hard he swam....

He awoke with a nurse holding him to keep him from throwing himself out of the hospital bed. When he lay still, warm waves of pain washed over him, gradually subsiding. Through the gaps in the bandages that otherwise completely swathed his face and head he could see the white hospital ceiling dim with night again. It had been night when they had brought him into this room. There had been a day, and now it was night again. The lapse of time disturbed him vaguely; somewhere somebody had been awaiting him. His memories were a confused mixture of what had happened long ago and what had happened quite recently.

The terrible panic of the nightmare still lurked shadowy at the back of his consciousness. He felt the need to apologize for the disturbance he had made.

"Sorry," he whispered. "Didn't mean to wake up everybody..."

His mouth felt clumsy and shapeless, but he seemed to have all the teeth to which he was entitled. His chest hurt and there was pain all through his face, but his eyes were functioning properly. He thought, *Well, I can see and talk and eat, I guess. I'm alive. I've got arms and legs and a head. Man, have I got a head!*

"Aren't you ashamed of yourself, Mr. Wilson!" the nurse said severely. "A grown man, screaming like a baby!"

He looked up at her blankly. Then the doctor came into the room, paused at the table by the door, and approached the bed with a hypodermic.

"Just relax, Mr. Wilson, and I'll give you something to help you sleep....No, don't try to talk now. Just lie still, please. Nurse..."

The sting of the needle was insignificant against the other pain, but the alcohol, swabbed on the punctured skin, left a brief, cold memory behind it. He let the drug carry him away. It did not really matter that they had got his name wrong. It was not as if *he* didn't know who he was....

Suddenly it was morning and the nurse was in the room again, fussing with something at the dresser. He had past and present all sorted out now; he could differentiate old nightmares from new realities. At one time in his life he had escaped from a wrecked and burning ship; at a later time he had escaped from a wrecked and burning automobile. The first occasion was quite clear in his mind. They had given him a medal for it. The second occasion was not quite so clear; he could not remember everything that had happened, and even the parts he could remember seemed contradictory and confusing. He remembered a man in a light hat and coat, who had told a disquieting story that did not have to be true. He tried for the man's face, but could not make it come clear. He remembered waking up screaming and being called by a name that was not his.

"Nurse," he whispered.

"What is it, Mr. Wilson?" She laughed cheerfully. "You're in the Rogerstown Memorial Hospital, if that's what's worrying you?"

He hesitated. An instinct warned him to be careful. "What's the matter with me? My face?"

"Oh, you're going to be all right, Mr. Wilson," the nurse said, still working at the dresser. She was a middle-aged woman with a thick, competent body dressed in starched white. There was gray in her hair beneath the cap. "You just have a slight concussion and a few assorted cuts and burns and bruises, that's all. In a week or two you'll be almost as good as new,"

He suspected that his nose was broken, and he felt as if a mule had kicked him in the chest; but he had been in hospitals before, and he knew that there was never any use in arguing with this kind of professional optimism.

"Was there—was anybody else hurt?" he whispered cautiously, feeling his way.

"Why, no!" she said, clearly startled at the thought that this might be worrying him. "Why, did you think you'd hit somebody? There wasn't a soul around when the highway police got there. A farmer saw the fire and called them. They said you must have fallen asleep and driven off the road. You're a very lucky young man, Mr. Wilson. If the door hadn't opened and let you fall clear as the car rolled..."

Young lay still. He could remember now his last glimpse of Lawrence Wilson, leaning over him with the iron that apparently had been lying hidden behind the seat all the time they had been talking; even so, his mind would not at once grasp the enormity that the nurse's words suggested. *He tried to burn me! He knocked me out and tried to burn me in the car! If the door hadn't opened...*

The nurse turned dramatically to show him the bowl of flowers she had been arranging. "Aren't they lovely, Mr. Wilson?" she cried. "I think glads are the prettiest things! Here's the card."

She put it into his hand and, after a glance at the bright array of pink gladioli, he brought the card up into his limited field of vision. It was one of those comic cards you send to invalids, a cartoon of a little girl in a boat with violently shaking sails, captioned, *I was all a-flutter when I heard you were sick.* The card was signed, *Bunny.* He gave it back to the nurse; it took all his strength to hold it out long enough for her to take it. He was tiring and his thoughts were slow and muddy; and he could not seem to concentrate on the fact that he was in a hospital under the name of a man who had, for some unknown reason, tried to kill him; and that the man's girlfriend was sending him flowers and might even decide to pay a visit.

"Nurse," he whispered.

"Yes, Mr. Wilson."

"Have you—got my things?"

The nurse put the card back with the flowers. "Why, yes, they're right here," she said. "Except your clothes; I'm afraid you'd better not plan on wearing that suit again, Mr. Wilson. But here are your keys and your watch and your wallet. Your money's in the hospital safe downstairs; a hundred and fifty-six dollars and some change. That's right, isn't it?...Oh, you want to see the wallet?"

"Please," he whispered.

She put it into his hands: Lawrence Wilson's wallet, that he had been holding in his hands when Wilson struck him down. He wondered dully where his own had got to. The wallet might have been attributed to him by mistake, but the thin, curved watch on the dresser did not belong to him, either; nor did the keys in their pigskin zipper case. And the nurse had indicated that he had been brought here wearing a suit of some kind instead of his uniform. It was clear that he had not become Lawrence Wilson by accident; the other man had apparently, after knocking him out, changed clothes with him before rolling him off the road in the car. Young tried to work out the possible motives for this in his head; but nothing came except a kind of weak resentment that he had been so easy to take.

He studied the wallet in his hands and opened it idly as he tried to force his thoughts into some kind of constructive pattern. The little book of plastic-protected identification cards inside fell open under his clumsy fingers at the snapshot of a girl on a boat; he remembered that. He stared at the small figure in a blank sort of way; this was Bunny, who had sent him flowers. *Who had sent Larry Wilson flowers,* he told himself; *let's keep these identities straight.*

He remembered that his original impression of the girl in the picture had been of a kind of tomboyish innocence; strangely, she now seemed to have assumed a tough and predatory appearance, a small, lean, and catlike figure in her scanty bathing suit. She was the girlfriend of the man who had tried to kill him; the one person, according to the story, who had stuck by Wilson after he had been fired from his government job for unstated reasons that Young was now willing to accept as excellent.

Larry Wilson's girlfriend seemed to stare at him out of the snapshot with a flat and cruel and triumphant look, as if gloating over the injuries her man had inflicted upon him. One eye gleamed a little, wickedly. Her expression fascinated Young; it seemed as if the inanimate paper had come alive beneath its plastic covering. Then the wallet tilted a little in his hands, and suddenly all life went out of the image, leaving it gray and neutral, just a poor representation of an unknown girl in a bathing suit.

Young frowned and regretted it; it hurt his face. He moved the wallet experimentally, and watched the gleam come back to Bunny's left eye. He squinted along the paper and discovered the simple reason for the phenomenon: someone had written something on the back of the snapshot, causing little ridges in the photographic emulsion, one of which had caught the light in just the right way to give the picture its satanic look.

Glancing up, Young found that he was alone in the room; the nurse had left him briefly. He could hear her footsteps down the hall through the door she had left open. The photograph shared a plastic envelope with a card of membership in some yacht club. He slipped both out, and studied the snapshot, turning it over. The back was quite blank. There was not even a sign of erasure.

The effort of concentration was fast using up the last remnants of his strength; he lay back on the pillow, closing his eyes, feeling perspiration wet on his face beneath the bandages. Still lying there with his eyes closed, resting, he ran his thumb across the face of the picture. It seemed to him that he could detect the tiny ridges that his eyes had seen; it seemed to him also that the paper was heavier and less flexible than was customary for an ordinary snap-shot print. He opened his eyes and focused on the edge of the picture and found the faint mark of lamination where a second sheet had been neatly cemented to the back of the first, the edges later trimmed to leave no unevenness. By working a corner back and forth, he made the two papers separate; they had been sealed together with rubber cement. He parted them cautiously, leaving them still attached near the bottom, and read the penciled list of names that was revealed:

Shooting Star
Aloha
Marbeth
Chanteyman
Alice K.
Bosun Bird
Estrella

There was a cryptic notation opposite each name. His mind could make no sense of any of this. He was very near to passing out; and the nurse was coming back along the corridor. He pressed the two small rectangles of paper again—the rubber cement taking hold nicely—and returned the snapshot and its companion card to the plastic envelope, and the envelope to the wallet, and dropped back to the pillow dizzily as the nurse entered the room. She came to the bed, retrieved the wallet, and moved away.

"I'll put it over here, Mr. Wilson," she said.

There was something he had to say; something he had to do. After all, he was not Lawrence Wilson, and something had to be done about this. Without opening his eyes, he whispered, "I'd like to see the doctor."

"Dr. Pitt's already made his rounds," the nurse said. "Why, what—There isn't anything missing from your wallet is there, Mr. Wilson?" Her voice had sharpened. "I can assure you—I mean, the office always makes a list—"

"No," he breathed, "no, it isn't anything like that. Everything is fine. I'd just like to talk to him for a moment. The doctor." The nurse wouldn't do, he thought. She would think him delirious or crazy. Besides, if he told the nurse he would have to repeat the story to the doctor anyway, and he did not have that much strength. "Please!" he whispered.

"Well, he's tied up right now.... Mr. Wilson, are you all right?"

"I'm fine," Young breathed sarcastically. "I'm wonderful. *Please* will you—"

The room had started to go around him crazily. He closed his eyes more tightly, and the bed swung away with him; and he forced them open, and the motion stopped.

"Damn it," he said clearly, "will you—"

"I'll get him when he comes out of staff meeting," the nurse said. The promise was quick and insincere. "The minute he's free, I'll certainly tell him, Mr. Wilson. Now you want to rest because we've got a nice surprise for you. Your wife's coming in to see you this afternoon, just for a moment this first day, and you want to be all—"

"My wife?"

"Yes, she's been here several times asking about you. She drove over and is staying in town, she told me. I guess you don't live very far from here, do you? You must feel kind of silly, driving all the way down from New York to have an accident almost at your own doorstep.... Honest, I think your wife is the loveliest person, Mr. Wilson, and that's funny because I don't go for people with Southern accents as a rule.... No, that's quite enough talking for now. We've got to save our strength for this afternoon, don't we? Please, Mr. Wilson, if you insist on exciting yourself, I'll have to give you a sedative!"

The door closed behind her. Young sank back against the pillow and lay staring helplessly at the white ceiling, trying to think, but nothing came, and he fell asleep.

When he awoke, somebody was talking about him. He recognized the voice of Dr. Pitt. There had been some evidence of concussion, the doctor said, but the X-rays had shown no signs of skull fracture. Lacerations of face and scalp were healing normally and would probably leave no serious disfigurement; however, there might be a slight thickening of the bridge of the nose, as was usual in these cases. The patient had a badly bruised chest from being hurled against the steering wheel; but apparently no ribs had been broken. It was fortunate that the wheel had held up, the doctor said; he had seen instances of drivers impaled upon the steering column like insects on a pin.... Footsteps moved away from the bed. The low, professional murmur of voices continued for a while; then the door closed softly.

Young opened his eyes, found himself alone, and lay for a while wondering to whom the doctor had been speaking: apparently, from the tone and terminology used, another doctor. He rang the bell at the head of the bed.

"Oh, you decided to wake up at last, did you?" the nurse said playfully, coming into the room. She adjusted the bed for him and raised the blinds to let sunlight through the windows. Then she went back to the door. "He's awake now, Dr. Henshaw," she said, and a large, balding, middle-aged man came in. He was wearing a brown suit, and even without the nurse's identification there would have been no doubt of his profession. In a hospital you could always tell; the doctors were the only men who seemed to feel really at home. Dr. Henshaw approached the bed briskly.

"Well, Larry, what do you think you've been doing to yourself, anyway?" he demanded. He did not wait for a response, but went on: "I've been talking your case over with Dr. Pitt, and he thinks you're well enough to come home and leave this room for somebody who's really sick, haha.... Nurse, will you have a stretcher brought up, please? And ask Mrs. Wilson to drive the station wagon around to the ambulance entrance...."

In his weakened, semi-drugged condition, it was difficult for Young to be sure of anything, but the voice stirred a sort of echo—of the Navy, of home...he wasn't sure.

He was given little time to think or to protest, and he found himself gripped by a strange indecision. He found that he had no real desire to convince these people of the mistake they were making. A moment later he no longer had a choice. There was a certain ruthlessness to which sick people were subjected when a decision had been made as to what should be done with them; in transit they were handled like a sort of perishable but inanimate freight: gently, even tenderly, but with efficiency and dispatch. In a moment, it seemed, he was being lifted into a large, shining station wagon from which all seats except the driver's had been removed to make room for a low cot, on which he was placed. Someone got in beside him and said in a clear, Southern voice:

"All right, Dr. Henshaw."

Then a girl's face moved into Young's field of vision, as the car started up beneath them.

"I reckon you must feel like you were being kidnaped, Mr. Young," the girl said, smiling.

It took him a while to realize that she had addressed him by his rightful name.

Chapter Three

He awoke gradually to the sound of a phone ringing somewhere in the house to which he had been brought. They had given him something when they put him to bed here and it had not quite worn off yet; he lay drowsily with his eyes closed, unready to move, but listening. Somebody came out of a room not far away and went downstairs to answer. The door to his room was apparently open; he could hear the quick, light footsteps receding down the stairs—the sound dulled by a carpet—and then the girl's voice speaking with the soft Georgia accent he remembered. He could not make out what she was saying to the person who had called.

The window of his room was also open. He could feel the breeze from it against the minor portions of his face not covered by bandages; and he could hear the sound of the occasional cars on the highway some distance away, and the faint field and woods noises that came quite clearly into the room although he knew himself to be on the second floor of the house. There was the buzz of an outboard motor on a body of water not too far away. *My wife…is staying at our place over on the Bay,* Lawrence Wilson had said. He had also said, *We haven't been getting along lately.*

Mrs. Wilson came back upstairs, entered Young's room, went past the foot of the bed to the window, and raised the Venetian blind. He opened his eyes.

"That isn't too bright, is it?"

He had the remote feeling of looking at someone on a distant stage; it took him a moment to realize that the girl was addressing a question to him.

"No," he whispered, "no, it's fine."

He watched from behind the shelter of the bandages as she came to the foot of the bed to look at him. He saw a slender, quite graceful, dark-haired girl apparently somewhat younger than his own age of twenty-nine. This morning she was wearing a long gold satin negligee that gave her a regal air; the effect was faintly marred, however, by the fact that her face was shiny and that her dark hair—somewhat longer than they usually wore it these days—was loose and a little untidy about her shoulders. It was clear that the telephone had awakened her, too. The lack of lipstick gave her face an unsophisticated and defenseless look.

"I declare, you haven't been lying here awake for hours?" she said quickly. "There's a bell right beside you, if you need anything, hear?"

There were at least two people in the house beside

himself, he decided; she, in the room with him, and somebody below, apparently in the kitchen. The dark-haired girl, clearly feeling his attention wandering, tried again.

"How do you feel this morning, Mr. Young?"

"Swell," Young said mechanically. "I feel fine."

"Bob—Dr. Henshaw says you can eat anything you like. Shall I have Beverly fix you some breakfast?" She laughed quickly. "I forget you don't know us. Beverly's the cook. Dr. Henshaw—well, you met him yesterday. He's the family doctor. I'm Elizabeth Wilson. We're all real respectable folks, and this is our"—she hesitated, and tried a smile that did not succeed—"our first kidnaping."

He was watching her hands, long and slender, gripping each other tightly as she faced him. The indirect sunlight from the window glinted on the rings—one displaying an impressive diamond—that would have reminded him, had he forgotten, who she was: the wife of a man who had tried to kill him; a girl who, knowing him not to be her husband, had nevertheless smuggled him out of the hospital and brought him here; a girl who knew his name. There was only one person from whom she could have learned it.

"Where is he?" Young whispered.

She glanced at him, startled. "Where is—?"

"Your husband."

She was suddenly quite still; and for a moment he

thought he saw in her eyes something gray and hopeless and lost, but the look vanished—if it had ever existed—and she laughed. "But how you do talk, Larry!" she murmured. "A person might think we weren't legally married, listening to you." She smiled at him, awaiting his protest, her slender hands still gripping each other tightly.

"But—"

"Honey, you're not going to give me a lot of trouble?" she said softly, rather breathlessly. "I'd hate to think we weren't going to get along.... I'll get your breakfast now."

She turned away. He watched her go out of the room; even in a hurry she had a nice way of walking. The satiny whisper of her golden robe seemed to remain for a while after she had gone.

Young shook his head minutely at some thought that was not quite clear. He listened to make sure she was safely downstairs. Then he sat up in bed. This was a cinch. There was nothing to it; it just hurt like hell in his chest and several other places. When he had caught his breath from the pain, he looked at himself in the mirror over the dresser.

The complete anonymity of the image that confronted him was disconcerting. He told himself dryly, *All you need now is a sheet and a length of chain to clank and you're in the business*. There was something ghostly and unnerving about the blank mask of bandages where a face should have been. Even with the eyes and the mouth showing, you could not help a dreadful little suspicion that there might not be anybody inside the stuff at all.

Young grimaced at his image in the mirror, which, except for a faint stirring behind the bandages, did not respond. He looked about the room, which had the look of a room in a very old house that had been quite well kept up for a while, but which had lately, for lack of money or interest on the part of the owner or tenant, been let go a little.

The wallpaper, still firm and fairly clean elsewhere, was blistered and discolored beneath the window where somebody's neglect had let rain get to it; the white calcimined ceiling was stained in one corner from a roof or plumbing leak above; the old, brown-painted wooden floor was worn to the bare boards by the bed and near the door.

It was clearly a man's room. The walls were hung with framed pictures of sailing yachts. A draftsman's table in the corner held the preliminary sketches of a small cruising boat. The paper had a limp, flat look that indicated that a long time had passed since it had been pinned there. Wilson had been driving down from New York, on his way to Washington, Young remembered; he had given the impression of a man who did not spend much time at home these days.

A naval architect by profession, he had apparently

made a hobby of designing sailboats in his spare time. It seemed like much too pleasant an occupation for a man who had done his cold-blooded best to murder a complete stranger. You wanted to think of the man who had tried to kill you as a perverted maniac, so that you could hate him properly; you did not like to think of him with a fine, if rather shabby, old house, and a beautiful, if rather enigmatic, young wife, and a room full of sailboat pictures that you wouldn't have minded owning yourself in the days before you got your fill of the sea and everything connected with it....

He had heard the car approaching without paying too much attention, vaguely expecting, if he had thought about it at all, that it would pass along the road above the house without stopping, as others had done. Then it was coming down the driveway fast, around the corner of the house, and pulling to an abrupt halt in the gravel, almost directly, it seemed, below the window of his room. As he started to push himself across the bed to look, the driver jumped out and up the steps to the front door with the unmistakable sound of high heels clicking against bricks or cement. He heard Elizabeth Wilson, downstairs, go to the door; and heard the sound of her voice raised in quick protest; then two people crossed the downstairs hall and mounted the stairs rapidly, almost running. There was a little scuffle in the corridor outside his room, as he slipped quickly back beneath the covers.

"Please!" Elizabeth Wilson's voice protested breathlessly. "I'm telling you, honey, he isn't awake yet!"

Another voice cried, "Well, it's about time he woke up then! What the hell's he got, sleeping sickness? Damn it, I tried to see him at the hospital and he was always too sick. And every time I call here you tell me he's asleep. Asleep, my foot! What kind of a show are you putting on around here, anyway, Lizzy? You didn't want any part of him when he was well; what's this loving-wife routine, anyway? Who're you trying to impress by making like Florence Nightingale? If Larry's well enough to come home, he's well enough to see me—" The voice, shrill and excited and quite young, ceased abruptly as the speaker entered the room. "Oh!"

Some instinct that he could not have explained made Young act out the part Elizabeth Wilson had prescribed for him. He opened his eyes now, and stared blankly at the ceiling for a moment; then, with the clumsy movements of a man awakening from deep slumber, he turned and raised himself a little to look questioningly in the direction from which the disturbance had come.

The small girl in the doorway was staring at his bandaged head with an expression of shock, temporarily silenced. Her face was quite familiar; it was the sharp young face from the snapshot in Lawrence Wilson's wallet. The photograph had not warned him that the girl would have red hair: it was cut quite short about her head. She was wearing a crisp green linen dress, immaculate white shoes and gloves that gave her a dressed-up, little-girl look. Young studied her, vaguely perturbed; she was not quite the person Lawrence Wilson and his snapshot had prepared him for. Somehow the situation, if not the picture, had led him to expect a woman. This was just a spoiled and willful kid, with the fair freckled skin that went with that coloring, and a thin, reckless mouth bright with orange lipstick.

Young glanced from her to the taller, dark-haired girl behind her. Elizabeth Wilson was watching him also, he realized, and with a desperate intensity that shocked him. Still in her satin robe, she had not yet found time to put on make-up; and the pallor of her lips emphasized the terrible whiteness of her face. She was looking at him, he saw, without hope, despairing; her slender hands were locked together in the prayerful little gesture he had already come to recognize as a signal of distress. There was unconscious pleading in every line of her body as she faced him; yet it was clear that she had no thought of influencing him now. Whatever she might have thought to accomplish in her own behalf by bringing him here, it was too late now; and she was simply waiting for his first words to bring down upon her the unknown disaster she could no longer hope to avoid.

The silence ran on. Elizabeth Wilson moved slightly; she put a hand against the door jamb to steady herself. He saw the sickness of fear in her eyes. Although he did not know the cause of it, it was a sickness with which he was only too familiar; it made the two of them suddenly akin, a different breed from the small, assured, redheaded girl between them. He looked at the visitor, and licked his lips, and heard himself speak.

"Hi, Bunny," he whispered.

Elizabeth Wilson drew a slow, gentle, unbelieving breath. The younger girl did not speak at once. When she did, her voice was a little too loud; it was clear that she was still disconcerted by the bandages.

"Hi, Larry," she said, and, still too loudly and brightly: "What the hell have you been doing to your head?"

He found himself imitating, in a sick man's whisper, what he could recall of Wilson's hearty manner of speaking. "Why, I was feeling kind of low, so I gave myself a couple of licks across the dome. Some guy told me it was supposed to make you feel good when you stopped. He was a damn liar." After a moment, he went on: "Thanks for the flowers, Bunny."

"It's all right," she said. There was a little uncertainty in her manner now, as if she found the situation developing in an unexpected manner. "Are you—all right, Larry?"

"Hell, yes," he whispered. "A broken nose, concussion, twenty-five stitches in my scalp, a couple of broken ribs…nothing to worry about, kid, nothing to worry about. Give me five years and I'll be as good as new." He chuckled. "Sure, I'm fine, Bunny. Everything's swell."

The girl flushed a little. "Well," she said, "well, pardon me for making a damn fool of myself, people." Her voice was shrill. "I just thought—Well, if *everything's* so damn *swell,* I'll just be running along!"

She looked from one to the other of them defiantly, as if daring them to laugh; then she whirled and was gone, and they heard the clatter of her heels, muffled, on the carpeted stairs. The front door slammed too loudly; and the car started up and went too fast up the drive, and along the road out of hearing.

In the room she had left, it was a long time before anyone moved. Then Elizabeth Wilson pushed herself away from the door jamb and walked stiffly across the room to the window. A full minute passed before she spoke.

"Why did you do it?" she asked then, softly.

"I don't know," he said.

"I'm grateful," she breathed. "Of course I'm very grateful. But I don't understand."

She did not look at him. Her eyes were focused on something outside, far away. Presently he raised himself in the bed to regard the view at which she was staring with such fixity. It was a pleasant view. Below the window, the lawn sloped away from the house to the crest of a steep, wooded hillside, that in turn plunged down to the shore, where he could just see, through the trees, a dock at which a good-sized power cruiser was moored. Beyond was the mouth of a river, opening into a body of water that, from its size, could be nothing but an arm of Chesapeake Bay. A cruising sailboat of moderate size with a dinghy in tow was just heading out of the river, close-hauled to the brisk southeasterly breeze; and a small powerboat with the low, narrow lines of the oysterman of this region was coming in, making good time with the wind astern.

The sunlight glinted on the sharp little waves out there. Young saw spray break, quick and white, against the sailboat's bow as she drove into the chop; the deck was gleaming wet forward and some stuff would be finding its way aft to the cockpit; everything would be secure below and the skipper would be laying out the expected day's run on the chart. It would be time for another cup of coffee, or perhaps the first beer of the day.... It was the first time he had looked at salt water for seven years, he realized. It gave him a queer feeling of nostalgia for which he was not prepared.

Preoccupied with these thoughts, he was hardly aware of the girl turning away from the window; then she was on her knees beside him, burying her face in the coverlet of the bed, her shoulders shaking beneath the bright satin of her dressing-gown.

"Oh, I can't!" she gasped. *"I can't!"*

"What is it?" he asked stupidly. "What's the matter?" She did not answer; and suddenly a few of the pieces fell together in his mind as he looked down at her tousled dark head, and he asked the question he had asked once before: "Where is he? Where's your husband, Mrs. Wilson?"

She lifted her wet face to him, kneeling there. Her voice was suddenly clear and almost steady. "He's...out there," she breathed. "Out there. Under the water. I killed him."

Chapter Four

"It was late at night when he came," she said quietly. "I'd been in bed for hours, trying to get to sleep. I don't reckon I've had a good night's sleep since Larry went away last year. Even if we didn't.... It's such a big barn of a house to be alone in."

Her voice trailed away. She was sitting on the edge of the bed quite close to him now. She stared straight ahead of her, unseeing; then she buried her face quickly in her hands.

"I declare, I've made such a mess of—of everything!" she gasped. "Everybody who has anything to do with me—nothing but trouble.... Larry, and Bob Henshaw, and now you.... If I had a scrap of decency, I'd shoot myself!"

Young came back to reality abruptly. She had had him fully with her, as an actress might have, a convinced and sympathetic audience; but this was phony tragedy. This was just a pretty woman wrapping up a situation in trappings of remorse and self-abasement that she did not feel but thought would go over well. It caused him to look at her critically as she sat there in an attitude of despair, her head bowed, her tumbled dark hair spilling over the hands that concealed her face.

He found himself suddenly noticing certain disillusioning details of her appearance that he had missed earlier, or discounted, because you always gave a beautiful woman the breaks, wanting her to be perfect. It shocked him a little to realize, now, that Elizabeth Wilson missed perfection by a significant margin, even when you made allowances for her emotional state and the early hour of the morning.

It was not just a matter of hair and make-up. The gold satin housecoat had made a fine impression on a man just awakening from drugged slumber; but at close range you could not help noticing that the regal garment had been worn at least once too often since its last trip to the cleaners.

There was even a small, but noticeable gap in the seam behind the left shoulder, once clumsily mended but opening again; and the bright cloth of the sash was dull and threadbare where it knotted at the waist. Also, Young noticed, the nail polish on the slender hands was badly chipped.... He stopped the inventory, suddenly ashamed, aware again of the odd sense of kinship that he had felt upon seeing the fear-sickness in her eyes.

For some reason, he remembered himself, a few

days ago, shaky and bleary and with cuts on his face where the razor had slipped, struggling grimly to pull himself together into a reasonable imitation of an officer of the United States Navy. Somehow the two situations seemed comparable to him, although he could not have said why this was so.

Elizabeth Wilson stirred, her face still hidden from him. "I've made such a mess of my life!" she whispered through the shielding hands. "I've just ruined practically everything I ever touched!"

It seemed to Young suddenly that he knew this slender, graceful, somewhat untidy, dark-haired girl very well, which was strange, not just because he had only met her yesterday—for practical purposes, only this morning—but also because he had not known any girl very well for several years.

But she brought back to him sharply everything he had learned about women at an earlier period of his life—and shore leave in wartime had been an effective education. He knew Elizabeth Wilson well enough already to accept her theatrical remorse for what it was, a kind of apology for the grim revelations she was about to make. Women could dramatize anything, apparently even homicide.

He grimaced at this, and spoke with deliberate brutality: "Never mind the mess you made of your life just now, Lizzy. Let's just hear about the mess you made of your husband."

It brought her around to look at him, shocked and indignant. They faced each other stiffly.

"Don't call me Lizzy," she whispered. This was irrelevant, and he did not respond to it. Presently she laughed somewhat sharply, and touched his knee. "I *was* kind of putting on an act for you, wasn't I, honey?"

"I had that impression, Mrs. Wilson."

"I do that," she whispered. "I know I do; I can't help it. It's—nice to have someone around who can see through it. Larry never did. Even after he began to hate me, I could still—"

This was getting them nowhere, either, and he had no strength to waste on it. "He came here that night?"

"Yes, of course," she said, and glanced at Young. "I *am* beating all around the bush, aren't I, honey? It's—it's so hard to—If I could only see your face! I—I can't tell at all what you're thinking of me."

"Never mind my face," Young said, but his voice was gentler than it had been. Unlikely as it seemed, he had forgotten the bandages. You had to admit, he thought, it was tough on a girl to have to make her confession, not only to a stranger, but to a stranger hidden behind an expressionless mask of surgical gauze. "Carry on," he said.

She hesitated. "I was glad to see him," she whispered, averting her eyes. "Honest. I was so—so lonely. When you've been married, even if it doesn't work.... I thought he must have come back to—to try to make it up between us, somehow; and I was glad, you understand! What did I care about his silly politics, anyway; and maybe I'd even been wrong about them. I—I wanted him to tell me I'd been wrong, that I'd made a terrible mistake, that I'd done him a terrible injustice, but that he was willing to forgive me. I—I dropped the gun on the table by the stairs and ran across the room to him, hoping he'd take me in his arms and—and kiss me—"

"Hold it," Young said, "Let's go back. You had a gun?"

She licked her lips. "I'm telling this all wrong, aren't I? Yes, I had a little gun. Larry himself had given it to me after we were married. This is kind of an isolated place, and when he was commuting to Washington he sometimes didn't get home till late. Sometimes he'd stay over all night."

Young said, "Okay, you had a gun. Now, what made you take it with you when you went downstairs to greet your husband?" It was becoming hard for him to concentrate, but instinct warned him that he had to get this all now. She was ready to talk about it now; she might never be again.

"Why, I didn't know it was Larry!" she said, surprised. "I was scared to death. I thought— All I knew was that somebody was in the house. Downstairs. I just lay in bed and shivered, hoping they'd go away and not come up, but they didn't go away. There were all kinds of crashing and rattling. I couldn't imagine what was going on. At last I couldn't stand it any longer. I got the gun and slipped down the stairs.... He was drunk," she breathed. "That's what he was doing, getting drunk and falling over the furniture. He—he laughed at me. He said—people were getting wise to the way the world was going and everybody was trying to jump on the nice, Red bandwagon; but that lots of people were going to find that there wasn't room, and if I thought he was going to take me with him—"

"He was going somewhere?" Young interrupted.

Elizabeth Wilson nodded. "That's what he said. I didn't understand it, exactly; but somebody was coming for him in a few days. If he hadn't been drunk, he wouldn't have talked so much, I guess; and if I hadn't—hadn't acted so glad to see him—" She shivered a little at some memory. "He even relented a little. He said that if...if I was a good girl and kept him hidden here without letting anybody know, and co-operated, he'd see what could be done about letting me come along."

"Did he say where he was going?"

"Not exactly, but it was out of the country—"

"Did he say how long he was going to have to wait?"

"Several days, at least. He didn't seem quite sure of that himself." Her hands were tightly clasped together in her lap now. "Then he began to boast," she whispered. "He said I didn't know he was in the Navy, did I? He said I didn't know his name was David Martin Young, Lieutenant, U.S.N.R.; and he pulled on the jacket he had taken off—"

"Blouse," Young said mechanically.

"—and strutted up and down in front of me. I didn't know I was a widow, he said; and told me about you. He had arranged things so nobody would miss him, he said; if anybody started looking, it would be for a stray Navy Lieutenant. Lawrence Wilson had died in a terrible accident and would be buried in the family plot in the Bayport Cemetery. If I really wanted to show that my heart was in the right place, I would go over and identify the body right, when they called me; in fact, that was what he had come here for, to make real sure I made the proper identification. If I didn't, if I tried anything, if he was caught, he would make damn sure that people would think I was just as deeply involved as he was. He said, what could I lose? I could even change my mind about going—and he wasn't quite sure he could arrange it even if he wanted to—and still, just by saying a few words I would be the rich widow of the late Lawrence Wilson, at least until wealth was no longer allowed to exist for private purposes." She looked down at her clasped hands and was silent.

"Carry on," Young said gently.

She glanced at him. "That's Navy talk, isn't it, honey? Larry used to affect a lot of slang he picked up at—" She shivered abruptly. "I said no," she whispered.

"That wasn't very smart," Young said.

"No," she breathed. "It was real silly, I guess. I should have—played along. But I was so—so sick and ashamed.... He got mad, of course, perfectly furious. He hit me. I fell against the table and the gun dropped to the floor. I—I crawled over and got it. I p-pointed it at him and told him to get out. I said I would give him until morning to get away from here, because he was my husband, and then I was going to call the police." She licked her lips. "It wasn't a very—dignified scene. I told him if he wanted help to go to his redheaded girlfriend; and he told me how funny I looked giving him orders, sitting there in the middle of the rug with my nightie up around my neck. He laughed at me and walked up to me and reached for the gun and—and I shot him. Maybe I thought he was going to kill me. Maybe I really hated him then. Anyway, I shot him."

Her voice stopped, and there was no sound in the room. Outside, a large insect of some kind blundered against the screen, and an outboard motor buzzed industriously on the river. Elizabeth Wilson rose abruptly, her hands still gripping each other desperately.

"I called Bob Henshaw," she said. "He—we got *it* down to the boat. There was an old chain lying on the dock—" Her throat worked. "...burned the rug and my nightie—it was all over rust and blood—while Bob took *it* out....Then the telephone rang. It was the Rogerstown General Hospital. They told me"—she licked her lips—"they told me that my husband—that my husband had been in an accident, but was going to be all right." She sank down on the bed again. "They said not to worry—not to worry."

Then she turned to him, and he held her as she cried. He was tired, and his face hurt, and she had forgotten in her misery that he was a badly bruised man who should be treated gently. But he did not mind. He did not mind the pain, or the awkwardness, bandaged as he was, of holding in his arms a weeping girl, practically a stranger, who was not fully dressed, or even the uneasiness of wondering—as you could never help doing when they spun you one of these long, sad yarns—just how much of the story it was safe to believe. He did not mind because, for the first time in more than seven years, he was concerned with the troubles of someone other than himself. But then he was getting drowsy again, and not even the excitement of Elizabeth in his arms could keep him awake.

Chapter Five

He awoke slowly, to the sound of voices. It seemed to him that he spent all his time awakening, these days, although he could never quite recall the circumstances of going to sleep. Bright striped sunshine was entering the room through the Venetian blind, and he was hungry. A subdued conversation was being conducted in the hall outside his room; by listening attentively he could distinguish the words clearly.

"The Decker girl?" This was a man's voice, oddly familiar. For a moment Young could think of only one man around here whose voice he might recognize—a man who was dead—and his breathing stopped and the little hairs rose along the nape of his neck. Then he realized that this was just the doctor, whose voice he had heard in the hospital the previous day. "You let *her* in here?" Dr. Henshaw was demanding incredulously. "Elizabeth, what were you thinking—"

"*Let* her!" The girl's voice was sharp. "The brat almost knocked me down and stepped on me. She was up the stairs before I could do a thing to stop her."

"But—"

"Honey, I was ready to die! But he came through for us, he really did. He called her Bunny like he'd known her all his life, and thanked her kindly for the flowers she'd sent to the hospital. You should have seen her face: I declare, she turned positively green! She could have scratched my eyes out! She thought he was Larry, of course; and I reckon it looked to her like I'd managed to make up with him somehow and turn him against her. She stamped out of here and slammed the door so hard I thought the house was going to fall down."

There was a brief silence. Then the doctor's voice said reluctantly, "Well, I suppose that's all right, then, and no harm done. In fact, having her see him and talk to him is the best possible thing that could have happened, since it worked. If she's convinced, certainly nobody else is going to have any suspicions."

The conversation moved away down the hall. Presently the doctor returned alone and entered the room. Hearing him approaching the bed, Young stirred, and for the second time that day went through his impersonation of a man waking up.

The doctor set his bag on the bedside table and looked down at his patient. "I am sorry to have to disturb you, Mr. Young," he said. "But this was my only free time today; and I thought I'd better take the opportunity to check how you were getting along. How do you feel this afternoon?"

"Fine," Young said, rather thickly. His face felt stiff and awkward beneath the bandages. "Hungry."

"Mrs. Wilson's down in the kitchen getting you something to eat." Dr. Henshaw was shaking down his thermometer and did not glance aside. "She says you had a bit of excitement here this morning."

Young whispered, "Well, a little redheaded kid came barging in, all worked up about something, if you call that exciting."

"Um," the doctor said, regarding the instrument in his hand skeptically. "I understand you handled the situation quite well."

"I'm glad you approve, Doc."

"Very few medical men like to be called Doc, Mr. Young."

"Sorry," Young whispered.

"I don't want to seem unduly suspicious," the older man said, frowning at the thermometer. "Naturally, we're grateful that you didn't give us away. But I'm curious about your motives, Mr. Young. Why did you let the young lady believe you were Larry Wilson? Come to that, why didn't you declare your identity at the hospital?"

Young moved his shoulders briefly. "In the hospital, I didn't have much of a chance before you snatched me out of there. Most of the time I was out cold. I did try to talk to the nurse, but she just shushed me like they do."

"And this morning?"

"Well," Young whispered, "let's say it just didn't seem like the right time to upset the applecart."

The doctor turned toward the bed. His voice held no particular expression. He might have been inquiring about a minor symptom. "How do you feel about it now, Mr. Young?"

"I don't know," Young whispered. "I guess I haven't made up my mind yet."

Everything was on a very calm and polite level of conversation, and the doctor bent over him and said, "Open your mouth, please," and inserted the thermometer and glanced at his watch. Straightening up, he regarded his patient for a moment, then turned away and walked around the bed to the window. He spoke to the sunlight outside.

"I don't know exactly what Mrs. Wilson told you," he said quietly. "She tends to be—well, she's a sensitive person. She feels things very deeply, Mr. Young. It has—made my task of protecting her rather difficult." He was silent for a period of time; then he went on: "The facts, I think, speak for themselves. You have reason to know her husband's character; he was a violent, ruthless man, and we suspect that he was also a traitor to his country, although that is an accusation I prefer not to make against any person without absolute proof, which I do not have in Larry's case. How Elizabeth came to marry him is neither here nor there; suffice it to say that it was a wartime marriage which she has had cause to regret—not that she has ever told me so, but I have eyes, Mr. Young, I have eyes. He came here that night, as you know, with blood on his hands—your blood, Mr. Young. It is clear that he expected to be able to bully her into helping him to escape. When she refused, he became furious. There was a scuffle in which a gun was involved. The weapon was discharged somehow. Mrs. Wilson says she fired it; I doubt that she really knows how it came to be fired."

His voice ceased. He glanced at his watch, came around the bed, removed the thermometer from Young's mouth, read it, and put it down without comment. Then he returned to the window.

"You know that she called me," he said, looking out. "I came, and sized up the situation, including her ability to stand up to questioning. She told me how Larry had already arranged for himself to be 'killed' in an accident many miles from here. It seemed too good an opportunity to dismiss; it seemed as if Fate had played a grim joke on Larry Wilson, letting him plan the official details of his own death. All that was necessary was to get rid of the body, which I did. It was—not an ethical act, by the standards of my profession, but sometimes the man takes precedence over the doctor, Mr. Young." Henshaw cleared his throat. "We made one mistake.

We failed to allow for the fact that Larry, having arranged to substitute a dead body—your dead body—for himself, had failed to make the body, shall we say, quite dead enough. Imagine our feelings, Mr. Young, when, after disposing of one Larry Wilson, we suddenly found ourselves with another on our hands, and that one an imitation! Fortunately for us, you were too badly hurt to speak out at once. There was only one thing to do; and we took you out of the hospital at the earliest opportunity and brought you here, hoping that, since you had no reason to love Larry Wilson, we might somehow persuade you.... Do you have a price, Mr. Young? We can afford to pay a reasonable amount."

The last words were spoken in a different tone, quite abruptly. Young looked up. "Price?" he asked. "For what?"

"For doing what you have already done once this morning. For impersonating Larry Wilson until we can arrange for you to leave in a manner that will not arouse suspicion. "As long—" The doctor made a sharp little gesture with his hand. "Don't you see, Mr. Young? It is a very simple proposition. As long as Larry Wilson seems to be in this house alive, his wife cannot possibly be suspected of having shot him."

Young did not speak at once and a little silence followed. Young watched the man at the window. Dr. Henshaw was wearing the rough brown suit of the day before, badly in need of pressing. It did nothing to flatter his heavy figure. The condition of the pockets of his jacket indicated that he was in the habit of shoving his hands into them deeply. He did so now.

"She's a wonderful person, Mr. Young," he said. "When I think of the way she has been treated here—! I would do anything to protect her, Mr. Young, anything!"

His voice was impressively sincere. Young studied him, feeling a certain respect, and also a certain pity, because you could never take quite seriously the feeling of a bald and middle-aged man for a girl twenty-odd years his junior. Yet this man had apparently loved well enough to put his career and reputation on the line for Elizabeth Wilson when she needed him. It was a thing not every man would do for the woman in his life, Young reflected; the old boy must have something on the ball, even though he didn't look it.

"Anything!" Dr. Henshaw said softly. "I would even let an innocent man be punished for a crime he did not commit."

Young looked at him sharply, and the doctor swung around to face him. "What do you mean?" Young demanded.

"It should be plain enough," the doctor said. "I do not know your motives for keeping quiet about your identity, *Lieutenant* Young, but I think I can make a fair guess at them. You were on your way to Norfolk to report for duty, were you not? And then, suddenly, you found yourself in the hospital under another man's name.... Are there, perhaps, reasons why you would prefer not to go back into the service, Lieutenant?"

"Listen—"

Henshaw waved the interruption aside. "No, your motives don't really concern me, Lieutenant. I don't think you are quite sure of them yourself, as a matter of fact; you've just been letting yourself drift with the tide, have you not? Well, I am suggesting that you keep right on drifting in the same direction, Lieutenant. It's fair enough. We will keep your secret if you keep ours. But let me warn you; Mrs. Wilson's welfare comes first with me. If you do anything at all to endanger her, I promise you that I will see you arrested, not only for desertion, but for murder." The doctor leaned forward slightly to emphasize his words. "Consider your position, Mr. Young. You are the man who was found in Lawrence Wilson's wrecked car, wearing his clothes, with his watch on your wrist and his wallet in your pocket. Who is going to believe that Larry Wilson—whose family has lived around here for generations—staged an unprovoked attack on a stranger he'd picked up along the highway, changed clothes with this man, and then came running home to be shot to death by his own wife? Do you think the police will pay any attention to this crazy yarn, when the logical theory is that it was the hitchhiker—a man panic-stricken at the thought of being called back into the armed forces—who murdered Wilson for his car and clothes and money, and then, perhaps injured in the struggle, cracked up the car trying to get away. Think it over, Mr. Young."

Chapter Six

The remainder of that day was a jumble of confused impressions with which Young did not try to cope, taking refuge in sleep, real or pretended. Then, suddenly, it was morning again, he was alone in the sunlit bedroom, and his mind was refreshed and clear. He could no longer avoid the thought that was clamoring for his attention.

"Deserter," he whispered, fitting the ugly word to his tongue. This was the real edge to Dr. Henshaw's threat. The notion of being accused of murder was too unreal to be taken quite seriously; but this was a charge that he could not honestly deny, remembering his indecision in the hospital, and his readiness here to play the role Elizabeth Wilson had desired of him. He might never have consciously decided not to report for duty; but he had certainly been quick enough to lose himself in another man's identity when the opportunity offered.

Yet the idea had a fantastic quality; it was something he had never considered, even back in the bad days after his release from the hospital when it had seemed they were about to send him back to sea again. He had considered throwing himself on the mercy of the medical authorities, and he had on one occasion toyed with the thought of shooting himself, but it had never occurred to him to think of deserting. The war's end had saved him then. When, a few weeks ago, he had received orders back to active duty he had gone out and got thoroughly plastered, but he had not dreamed of not proceeding and reporting as ordered. Yet the germ of the notion must have been somewhere in his mind, he reflected, for him to slide so readily into acceptance of the present situation....

He sat up abruptly. *Acceptance, hell!* he thought, with sudden anger. Listening, he could hear sounds of activity from the kitchen downstairs, but nothing moved on the second floor of the house. He threw the covers aside, swung his feet to the floor, and stood up cautiously. The problems of operating in a vertical rather than a horizontal plane took a little consideration, but he ventured the three steps from the bed to the dresser without meeting disaster. From there he made it to the nearby closet door. Opening this, he studied the clothes inside. There were not very many of them; apparently Lawrence Wilson had removed most of his personal belongings when he left. Nevertheless, enough remained to dress his successor adequately; and it had already been established, Young reflected, that Wilson's garments would fit him. After all, he had been wearing one of the man's suits when the police had picked him up, half dead, at the scene of the wreck.

He frowned, his mind busy with feverish plans for escape. He was not aware of the girl's presence until her soft, Southern voice addressed him from the doorway.

"Honey, whatever are you doing? You're supposed to stay in bed, hear?"

He turned, startled, to face her. She was wearing the somewhat tarnished gold robe that seemed to be her usual morning costume, and her dark hair was no tidier than it had been the morning before, but her mouth was red with fresh lipstick. She was holding a large tray with breakfast for two. When he did not move or speak, she came forward and set the tray on the dresser. She looked up at him, standing there.

"I declare, you're bigger than I remembered. It's no wonder we had trouble getting you up the stairs the other day."

Her appearance and attitude disconcerted him. He found himself, unwillingly, aware of the graceful shape of her body beneath the satin negligee, and of the small, promising fullness of her lower lip. It was hard to look upon her as a jailer.

He said, "I can't stay here, Mrs. Wilson."

Her eyes widened slightly. "Why not?"

"The Navy'll be looking for me."

"Let them look, honey. They won't come here. You're Larry Wilson now, remember."

He said, "That's not precisely what I meant."

She hesitated. "Oh, I see. You've changed your mind. You want to go back?" Her voice was flat. She glanced at the open closet door. "You were looking for some clothes to run away in, honey? That's why you're up?"

He nodded.

She regarded him for a moment longer, then said, "Why, you don't have to run away, honey. The telephone's right at the foot of the stairs. You can call them right now if you like. I declare, you're big enough. I couldn't do a thing to stop you. If you *want* to see me put in prison—" Her voice trailed away. She faced him a little defiantly, her shoulders square and her head well back.

There was, he told himself, no reason why he should consider this girl in making his decision. Yet it was an added complication, and beneath the weight of it his strength and resolve began to crumble. He found himself swaying a little, and steadied himself against the dresser; then Elizabeth Wilson was beside him, helping him back to the bed.

"You do what you think is right, honey," she said breathlessly. "I declare, I wouldn't want you to get into trouble on my account. And don't pay any attention to Bob Henshaw and his threats, hear? He told me what he'd said to you yesterday and I was perfectly furious with him. I hope you don't think I'd let him do anything like that, even to save me. If you feel you've got to—to sacrifice me to your conscience, honey, you just go right ahead."

Her voice was sweet and wholly insincere, yet her nearness was pleasant and reassuring. He caught her arm as, after tucking the covers about him, she started to rise. She stopped talking and looked down at him quickly.

He said, "Elizabeth, you're a fraud. If I went near that phone, you'd probably shoot me."

The false cheerfulness slipped from her face like a mask, leaving it strained and pleading. "But you won't," she whispered. "You won't, will you, honey? You'll stay and help me. Won't you?" she whispered, and abruptly she raised a hand to her mouth and scrubbed it back and forth roughly, removing the fresh lipstick; then she kissed him without caution or restraint.

He was aware of the disturbing pressure of her lips and body; and he was not too weak to react to it, but she slipped away from him expertly as he tried to hold her, and stood up to look down at him, smiling. The smile gradually died away; and they studied each other for a long moment curiously, both clearly quite aware that a pact of sorts had been sealed.

"I declare," she said, "it would be real nice if I could see your face."

He said dryly, "Don't be too sure of that."

She moved her shoulders in a shrug that was less graceful than her usual gestures. "Well," she said, "well, we'd better do something about this breakfast before it gets stone cold."

He watched her turn toward the tray, the worn and soiled satin of her negligee swirling in a fluid way about her. He found that he could no longer look at her critically. They had suddenly become partners, accomplices in each other's crimes.

He said abruptly, "It was during the war. I was on a ship that was torpedoed. Ever since I've been allergic to ships and the sea and fire and the smell of gasoline. I've tried to lick it, but every time I think I'm getting somewhere it comes back again, as strong as ever. Hell, after my little encounter with your husband, I wound up having one of my nightmares again. I hadn't had one of those for four years."

She brought him a plate and set a cup of coffee beside him. "You don't have to tell me, honey. I declare, the uniform doesn't mean anything to me. I saw too many of them in Washington during the war, and the fellows inside them all had the same idea, about me. That's why I finally married Larry, I reckon; he was the one man I went around with who didn't have a uniform and couldn't act as if he thought his commission entitled him to bedroom privileges from every girl in Washington."

Young said, "It isn't just being scared, Elizabeth, although God knows I'm scared enough. It's—well, it's like this. I'm a lieutenant now; and I'd be up for lieutenant commander pretty soon. Well, a lieutenant commander probably didn't seem very much to you in Washington, but he can be a pretty big wheel on shipboard. And—well, I keep seeing myself on the bridge some dark night with the responsibility for a few million dollars worth of ship, maybe, and the lives of several hundred men and suddenly something happens, anything.... I don't know what I'd do, Elizabeth. I used to know, but I don't any more. I simply have no idea how I'd react. And I guess I really would just as soon not have to find out; I guess that's what it all amounts to, why I didn't tell them who I was in the hospital, why I let you and Henshaw bring me here."

She said, "Honey, eat your breakfast. I don't care, I tell you."

He looked at her where she was sitting on the edge of the bed now, eating off her knee; and he saw that she really did not care. She was not that interested in him. The fact that he intended to help her was enough. He found himself wryly amused at the thought that his personal tragedy could mean so little to someone else.

After she had left the room to take the tray downstairs, he got out of the bed again and moved around it to the window and looked out at the river and the Bay. They looked much as they had the day before; it was another nice day, with the same southeasterly breeze, apparently the prevailing summer breeze in this area. Far out, a sailboat was heading toward him wing-and-wing on a course that would eventually bring it into the mouth of the river below the house. Young wondered idly if this was the boat he had seen putting out the day before; presently, as it approached, he decided that this was a somewhat smaller craft. Something about it seemed vaguely familiar, reminding him of the picture Lawrence Wilson had shown him just before knocking him out, of the sloop he, Wilson, had designed for the girl called Bunny. The guess was confirmed when the boat came close enough for him to see that the small, solitary figure in the cockpit had red hair.

Bunny held her course clear across the river mouth to the near shore before she smartly put her helm down, brought the jib across, and trimmed sheets for the upriver reach. A thirty-foot sloop was not much boat by Navy standards, but it was still several tons of wood and metal, and several hundred square feet of canvas; a handful for a girl to manage. Young grimaced slightly; he did not like competent, athletic young women, particularly around boats; they always seemed to have a compulsion to demonstrate that they were just as good as men, or a little better. The kid was obviously showing off right now.

As she sailed past the big power cruiser moored at the Wilson dock, Bunny looked up at the house above. She must have seen him watching her from the window, because she raised a hand in greeting. Young hesitated, but it seemed better to wave back, and he did. The white sloop pulled away up the river, showing him the name lettered in gold leaf across the stern transom, too small to be read without glasses at this distance. He frowned at it, disturbed by a memory he could not immediately place. *Boats?* he thought, and then, with sudden understanding: *Of course! Boats!*

A sound behind him made him turn, to see Elizabeth standing there, regarding him a little oddly.

"Well, I declare, you're real friendly with the child!"

He glanced over his shoulder at the small white yacht now disappearing around the wooded point up the river, and he laughed. "What am I supposed to do when she waves at me, stick out my tongue? I'm supposed to be her old pal Larry Wilson, aren't I?"

Elizabeth did not smile. "I wonder what she was doing out there at this hour of the morning."

"Just sailing around, I guess," Young said, and dismissed the subject. "Tell me," he said, "where's that wallet?"

"What?"

"The wallet. Your husband's wallet. I had it in the hospital, with his keys and some other stuff. Where did it get to?"

"Why, it's in the top dresser drawer, honey," Elizabeth said. "What—"

He moved past her to the dresser, pulled the drawer open, and took the pigskin wallet over to the bed, sitting down to examine it. Elizabeth seated herself beside him.

"What is it, honey?" she asked in a worried tone. "What are you looking for?"

"I just got an idea," he said. He found the snapshot and looked at it for a moment. "What's her name?" he asked curiously.

"Why, you know that," Elizabeth said, surprised. "You called her Bunny yourself."

"I hope she wasn't christened that."

"It's really Bonita," Elizabeth said; and somewhat tartly: "That's a kind of fish, isn't it?"

"You're thinking of bonito," Young said with a grin. "Bonita what?" As he asked the question, he remembered Dr. Henshaw's reference to 'the Decker girl' the day before, but there was no need to admit that he had been eavesdropping.

"Bonita Decker," Elizabeth said. "Honey, why are you so interested in her, all of a sudden?"

He said, with some annoyance, "Damn it, if I'm going to be Larry Wilson, I ought to know my girl-friend's name, oughtn't I? Don't start spitting like a cat just because I ask a few questions. Actually, it's the picture I'm interested in at the moment. Watch now!" He separated a corner of the snapshot from the backing that had been so neatly cemented to it, and stripped the two small rectangles of paper apart with a flourish. "I spotted this in the hospital, but it had slipped my mind. Now, what's the name of the Decker girl's boat?"

"Why, she calls it the *Mistral,* I think," Elizabeth said, clearly puzzled by this performance. "But what—"

Young turned the photograph over, somewhat dramatically, to display the list of names written on the back. Her eyes widened with quick interest, and she leaned closer to look. They studied it together, Young paying particular heed, this time, to the lightly penciled notations opposite each name, that he had skipped over in examining the list hastily in the hospital while the nurse was out of the room.

Shooting Star, p, 28, N.Y.
Aloha, sl, 42, Newp.
Marbeth, p, 32, N.Y.
Chanteyman, k, 32, Jacks.

Alice K., sch, 40, Charleston
Bosun Bird, sl, 25, N.Y.
Estrella, p, 26, Wilm.

Presently Young drew a long breath and straightened up a little. "Well," be said, "it isn't there. No *Mistral.* So much for that idea. I don't know what it would have proved anyway."

Elizabeth glanced at him. "Honey, I don't understand. What is it?"

"It's obviously a list of boats," he said. "With descriptions. *Shooting Star,* power boat, a twenty-eight footer, hailing from New York. *Aloha,* sloop, forty-two feet, Newport…'k' means ketch, I suppose, and 'sch' is schooner. Jacks is Jacksonville and Wilm is Wilmington. That much is pretty clear sailing, I think. But what the hell it means is something else again." He frowned. "There's a connection somewhere. Your husband spent a lot of time on that girl's boat last summer, didn't he? I got that impression from what he told me."

"He certainly did!" Elizabeth's voice was edged. "I declare, I never was so humiliated in my life. I wouldn't—wouldn't have minded so much losing my husband to another *woman,* but to a nasty child and a sailboat!"

Young glanced at her. It amused him to say, dryly, "According to him, you weren't particularly eager to keep him after that Washington business."

She flushed. "Well, I certainly wasn't going to let anybody think I sympathized with his politics. But—but he didn't have to go ahead and make a fool of himself in public, spending all hours of the day *and* night—"

"Maybe he wasn't making quite such a fool of himself as you thought," Young said.

She glanced at him quickly. "What do you mean?"

"Well, it's got to tie in somehow," Young said. "He gets fired from the Navy Department for subversive activities. He immediately goes to work on the Deckers' boat, designing, building, and sailing the thing. Did he give any reason?"

She moved her shoulders briefly. "He said—I don't remember exactly. Something about taking up yacht designing in a professional way, and this was a start. He said a designer can make his reputation on one good fast boat that wins a lot of races; and *Mistral* was going to be it, for him."

"Did he need the money?"

She shook her head quickly. "Heavens, no! There's plenty of money, thank God; it's the only thing that—that's made my life here at all bearable, even before I learned—what he was doing."

"You mean, he didn't need his government job either?"

She shook her head again. "Oh, no," she said. "He just started doing it during the war, and liked it;

anyway, that's what he said. He said having money is no excuse for a man's sitting around on his can all day; that's the way he put it. I believed him; why shouldn't I have? It wasn't until they fired him that I—that I began to think of little things that had happened, phone calls, people he'd go out to meet in the middle of the night....I didn't *want* to turn against him when everybody else—But he didn't need my help," she said bitterly. "He didn't want it. He had—her."

Young said, "She's just a kid."

Elizabeth laughed. "Honey, she's not *that* young; she graduated from college last spring. I declare, I feel kind of sorry for her. She's a spoiled rich brat with a lot of wild political ideas; and she's had a crush on Larry since she was in diapers. I've had to listen to heaven knows how many stories about the way she used to trail him around when they were kids; he was six years older, of course. I don't think she knew what she was getting into; I think he sold her a bill of goods."

Young said, "Well, it sounds reasonable; but the question still remains, just what the hell was he after? What's the name of the boat down at the dock?"

"Larry's boat? That's the *Amberjack.*"

Young glanced at the list again. "She's not there, either. Yet here are the names of seven boats that he considered important enough, for some reason, to keep with him, hidden in this fancy way. And he came here for his getaway, don't forget that."

Elizabeth looked startled. "Why, what does that have to do with—"

"Why did he take the risk of coming here, Elizabeth? Why did he want you to hide him here? Why did he show himself to you at all? He'd just committed a murder to make it look as if he were dead; why risk blowing the whole scheme apart by letting you know he was alive?"

"He said he wanted to make sure I identified the body—"

"If I'd burned up in the car as he'd planned, you'd have given the body one quick glance, lost your lunch, and then identified it as him on the strength of the wrist watch and belt buckle. Anyway, it was a better gamble for him than coming here to put pressure on you. No, I think he came here for another reason. I think he came here to catch a streetcar. A seagoing streetcar. All these boats mean something; and I think friend Wilson knew that one was coming here and was going to make you hide him out until it came to pick him up, after which he would either have taken you along or disposed of you in some plausible manner to keep you from talking. But he had to have a hiding place close by, because he didn't know exactly when to expect his transportation. Small boats can't keep an exact schedule; a storm will keep them in port for a week—" Young's voice trailed off. The list in his hand stared up at him: *Shooting Star, Aloha, Marbeth, Chanteyman....* Boat names were never long on originality, he reflected sourly. *Bosun Bird, Alice K., Estrella.*

As he looked at the list, and remembered the character and suspected connections of the man among whose belongings it had been found, he began to see frightening implications in the commonplace names. *A bunch of small, innocent-looking pleasure yachts puttering up and down the coast under secret orders.... You don't know,* he told himself, *you're only guessing.*

"Damn it!" he said aloud. "I wish I'd never—" He did not finish the thought. The girl beside him did not speak. After a while he said uncertainly, "Elizabeth, we really ought to—"

"What?"

He did not look at her. "Let the F.B.I. know about this."

"Honey," she said softly, "honey, are you plumb crazy?"

"But listen," he said, "we don't even know how many there are! I mean, this list of seven. Hell, it doesn't *have* to be all of them. He might just have scribbled down the names of the ones he expected to be somewhere in this area at this time. Suppose there are hundreds of the damn little—"

"Honey, stop it!" She was on her feet, facing him. "Stop it!" she snapped. "I declare, it's a little late for you to get an attack of patriotism, isn't it, *Lieutenant* Young?"

"But we can't—"

"Oh, can't we?" she cried, and before he could guess what she was about to do, she had snatched the picture out of his hand and torn it across. He came to his feet, reaching for the pieces, and she turned away from him and, as he grabbed at her, jabbed an elbow accurately and hard into his bruised chest. The pain took his breath away. He gagged and sat down heavily on the edge of the bed, hugging himself, very close to being sick but distantly aware that she had run out of the room. He heard the toilet flush in the bathroom across the hall.

"Honey," she said, returning, "honey, I'm sorry. I declare I didn't mean to hurt you, but heavens, that silly conscience of yours—"

"It's all right," he said wearily. "It's all right, Elizabeth."

"You're not going to—"

She was interrupted by a noise outside. Below the window, a car door opened and closed with a weighty, deliberate sound, although, preoccupied with their own affairs, they had heard no car drive up. Elizabeth wore a look of panic, and Young knew exactly what she was thinking: Dr. Henshaw was not due to look in again until late in the afternoon. She caught Young's arm and moved fearfully to the window beside him. Looking down, they saw a long black Packard sedan of prewar orgin standing in the graveled circle in front of the house. An impressive elderly lady, who walked with the aid of a heavy cane, was just mounting the steps to the front door.

As they stood there, frozen, the visitor gave three imperative raps on the knocker and stepped back, leaning her weight upon the cane, to look up at the house. They pulled back from the window quickly, before she could see them.

"Oh, Lordy!" The despair in Elizabeth's voice took any humor from her whispered exclamation. "It's old Mrs. Parr! What's she doing here?" Then she turned on Young, grasping at him fiercely with both hands. "What are we going to do, honey? *What are we going to do?*"

The expression on her face startled him with its sudden naked terror; and he knew again the strong feeling of kinship that he had experienced before with this girl. It had become an emotion now, very close to tenderness; the affection and sympathy he could not help but feel for someone whose weakness he understood and shared, with the difference that his particular allergy—if you could call it that—did not react very strongly to an old woman with a cane.

He could not free himself from her without using

force, so he put his hands on her hips instead and pushed her gently back a little and held her steady in front of him.

"Easy now," he said. "Snap out of it, Liz." She stared at him blankly. "Who is she?" Young demanded. "What do I call her?"

Below, the knocker sounded again; and the girl's body jerked at the sound. *"But you can't—"*

"What the hell did you hire me for?" he whispered. "Now wipe your nose and get that stupid look off your face, sweetheart! What do I call this ancient character? Brief me; fill me in! Is she an old friend of the family, or what?"

"She—" Elizabeth shivered, and released him, and drew her sleeve across her mouth. "She's your—Larry's—"

"Mine," he said. "I'm Larry. Don't forget it. Carry on."

"She's your aunt. I mean, she isn't really your aunt; she's some left-handed kin to the Wilsons that I never did get straight, but you call her Aunt Molly. *I* call her Mrs. Parr." Elizabeth had recovered enough to be bitter about this. "That is, that's what I call her when she can't avoid letting me speak to her; it hurts any of the family to admit that I exist. I declare, I think they even blame me for what Larry—I can't imagine what would make her visit—Oh, shut up, you old biddy!" she gasped, as the knocker rapped again.

Young asked, "Where's the maid? Why doesn't she answer it?"

"Who? Oh, Beverly. She only comes once a week; I can't stand having them around the house. I don't know how to—They always make me feel like poor white trash, the way they look at—"

"Let's save your inferiority complexes till we have time to analyze them properly. Mrs. Parr, sweetheart, Mrs. Parr!"

Elizabeth licked her lips. "Well, she lives at a place called Laurel Hill, way up the river. Larry—you took me there in the *Amberjack* once. It's a museum place with antiques and everybody says it's simply marvelous, although I declare, it looked like a junk shop to me. Don't let her get started on it or she'll be here all morning.... Oh, God, I look a wreck!" She had turned to the mirror now. "She's going to think I always trail around the house like this!"

She smoothed her hair. Young was climbing into bed.

"Never mind that," he said. "Get the hell down there before she starts hammering with that cane; and for God's sake be nice to the old battle-ax.... Elizabeth?"

She turned at the door. "Yes?"

"Chin up, as the British say. Don't give up the ship, and stuff."

She managed a smile. "Honey, you're sweet! I'm all right now."

Young watched her dubiously as she moved away. Then he grimaced beneath the bandages and settled himself against the pillows and smoothed the covers over him. It occurred to him, belatedly, that he should have let down the Venetian blind, not only to give the proper sick-room atmosphere, but also to lower the visibility somewhat; but it was too late now. He could already hear the murmur of voices at the front door. When they disliked each other thoroughly, women had a way of being nice to each other that you could recognize even when you were so far away that you could not distinguish the individual words.

Presently the cane thumped deliberately on the carpeted stairs, and a deep, almost masculine, voice said, "...intrude at this hour, but I didn't realize how early it was. Why, you've just barely got up, haven't you, dear?"

Elizabeth's voice said, "Oh, Larry'll be delighted to see you, Mrs. Parr. The poor boy's getting so bored with staying in bed that just talking to anybody is a real treat."

Young grinned to himself, and stopped grinning; there was a little moment of extreme tension before they showed in the doorway. *Okay, junior,* he thought, *you're Larry Wilson now. I'm Larry Wilson now*.... Then the old lady was standing there, not allowing herself to lean on the cane, but getting as much unobtrusive support from it as she could while she caught her breath from the climb. She seemed like quite a formidable person, a large woman fully turned out for visiting in hat, gloves, and a light summer coat open to show one of those elaborate print dresses that all wealthy elderly females seemed to wear. She looked at Young and chuckled.

"Well, Lawrence, they've sure enough got you wrapped up like a country ham," she said. "Bonita told me—"

"Oh," Young said. "She did, did she?"

"Hell, I wasn't supposed to let that out." Mrs. Parr showed no particular evidence of consternation or remorse. She gestured at Elizabeth. "Bring me that chair, dear. I recall telling this boy's mother a month before he was born that if she planned having any more than the one, she should do something about those damn stairs. But I never thought then I'd see the day when they'd give me trouble. Well, nobody stays young forever. Maybe it's just as well. Young people seem to be forever inventing new ways of getting themselves into difficulties." She seated herself gratefully in the chair that Elizabeth brought forward, and looked up at the girl. "And now I wonder if I could impose on you for a cup of coffee, my dear.

Of course, if you haven't started breakfast yet—"

Elizabeth flushed angrily. "Oh, we've eaten, Mrs. Parr, but I think there's still some coffee on the stove." Then she glanced quickly at Young. "It—won't take a minute," she said uncertainly.

"I hate to be so much trouble."

"Oh, it's no trouble at all." There was an edge of desperation in Elizabeth's voice, as if she were being pushed bodily from the room.

"Bring me one too, darling, while you're at it," Young said. Reluctantly she turned away. When she had gone, Young glanced at Mrs. Parr, who was patting her wrinkled, carefully made-up face delicately with a large handkerchief. In spite of the sheltering bandages, Young felt suddenly naked and helpless, facing her alone. There was so much he did not know, so many ways in which she could trap him, if she wished.

"I recall this room," she said absently, looking around. "You had it as a boy, didn't you?" He did not have to answer, because she turned her gaze on him immediately. "Now, what the hell is all this foolishness, Lawrence?" she demanded. "If you and that redheaded brat of Maude Decker's think you're going to involve me in any romantic shenanigans at my age— As far as your marriage is concerned, boy, I've got no sympathy for you at all. You've got a pretty wife. I suppose she doesn't spend all day in a wrapper and nightgown. Maybe you could have done better, but you didn't; and I've got no patience with the modern attitude toward marriage. In my day, a man was supposed to live with his mistakes. Don't come to me expecting me to set up assignations for you behind your wife's back!"

Young said, "I didn't come to you, Aunt Molly."

"Well, your girl did, damn it. She wanted me to help her arrange some kind of meeting.... Me carrying love notes at my age! Somebody should turn that child over and warm her bottom, and yours too, young man.... I don't know why I keep calling her a child. At her age I was married and keeping house for three children, a husband, and a pack of dogs. The dogs had the best manners of the lot. If anybody had suggested that I show myself in public in a pair of little pants and a bit of a handkerchief—! Anyway I told Bonita and now I'm telling you that I'll have nothing to do with it. Not that it will stop you, I suppose; I understand the two of you were carrying on something scandalous all last summer. Well, you get no sympathy from me, remember that. In my day, these things were conducted with at least a little bit of discretion.... I told the girl, 'Girl,' I said, 'don't come weeping to me because you got left out in the cold. What do you expect, playing around with a married man? If you want any messages carried, carry them yourself. Do I,' I asked her, 'look like Cupid to you, girl? So the boy got himself smashed up and his wife's looking after him and that's the way it should be. I'm certainly not going to tell him to give you the usual signal when he's well enough to walk out and can meet you at the usual place,' I told the chit, 'and I strongly advise you not to make a spectacle of yourself by sailing past the house twice a day, morning and evening, waiting to hear from him; and if you do go sailing,' I told her, 'for Heaven's sake put a few clothes on for a change.' Humph. Well, I've never had a very high opinion of human intelligence, and I suppose you'll find some damn fool or other to carry your messages for you....Lawrence."

"Yes, Aunt Molly," he said.

"I don't hear much up the river there, but somebody was telling me you had got yourself mixed up in this Communist nonsense. That isn't true, is it?"

"No, Aunt Molly," he said.

"Well, that's fine," she said. "I'm glad to hear it...Oh, there you are, my dear. You really shouldn't have gone to all this trouble for me." Mrs. Parr looked at Elizabeth critically as she brought a tray into the room. "That's a lovely robe, you're wearing, dear; it's a pity you seem to have got some lipstick on the sleeve. And I do love your hair like that; I think this modern style of whacking it all off short is most unattractive. In my day, her hair was considered to be a woman's crowning glory...."

Chapter Seven

The long Packard had to back up once to get around the circular drive, which had been laid out for vehicles of shorter wheelbase—no doubt originally for horse-drawn carriages. Then the big car made its deliberate way around the corner of the house and out of sight. Young turned from the window.

"Does she always drive that hearse herself?"

"She had a chauffeur before the war, Larry told me. When he got drafted, she got somebody to teach her to drive, and liked it so much she never hired another." Elizabeth swung about to face him. "Honey, what did she want? What did she say?"

He was tired now, and he got back into bed and leaned back against the pillows before answering. "Why," he said, "somehow she'd got herself talked into giving me a message from Bonita Decker, and she wasn't too enthusiastic about the idea, although I doubt it's going to keep her awake nights. The kid apparently hasn't given up hope. She wants to see me. She's going to sail past this place twice a day waiting for me to give her the usual signal, after which I'm supposed to sneak out and meet her at the usual place."

"A signal?" Elizabeth demanded. "What signal? What place?"

Young said, "How the hell would I know? I don't know the place, either; or the time. I suppose they had a standard time for meeting, since the old lady didn't bother to mention it. You had no idea they had some system like that rigged up?"

She shook her head. "I didn't pay much attention to his comings and goings last summer, but I declare, I didn't dream they—"

"Well, it looks as if they had really been taking this affair seriously. Signals and secret meeting places! I wish I knew.... Well, it doesn't matter. I obviously can't afford to meet her; that would be running this bluff into the ground. I may be able to fool an old lady who never saw Larry Wilson more than once a year; I'm sure as hell not going to get anywhere with a bright little girl who was in love with him, bandages or no bandages. And with the color hair she's got, if she doesn't get her signal pretty soon she's going to get impatient and send somebody else or come barging in again herself.... I think we'd better have Henshaw over here and hold a council of war, Elizabeth. This act is dying on us; we'd better wind it up before it folds completely. It's time for Larry Wilson to go to Nassau for his convalescence, or visit the Mayo Clinic for an operation, or something. We've established that the bastard's still alive; now let's get him the hell out of here."

She had turned to study her reflection in the mirror, in a preoccupied way. "All right, honey," she said. "But can't it wait until this afternoon? Bob said he'd be over."

"Oh, I suppose so." He could not explain his sudden feeling of urgency; instinct was warning him that the game was up, the gag was wearing thin, the ship was sinking beneath him.... He tried to put the last metaphor out of his mind, but it was like that; it was the well-remembered sensation of knowing that there were only so many seconds—in this case minutes, or maybe days—before the whole thing would go up with a bang and a hiss and a roar, taking him to hell with it if he had not vacated the premises by the time it happened. His mind was working swiftly and well. "Elizabeth," he said, knowing what he had to do now. It was time to demonstrate that he was keeping all possibilities clearly in mind.

She looked at him over her shoulder, clearly struck by something in his voice. "What is it, honey?"

"The gun," he said. "Have you still got it?"

"What?" she demanded, although he was sure she had heard.

"The gun you used that night. Have you still got it, or did you get rid of it?"

"Why—why, I've still got it, honey. Bob and I talked it over; people knew I had it, Larry had mentioned giving it to me, so it seemed better to hang onto it. If—if there were any questions, it would have looked funny for it to turn up missing. Bob—cleaned it for me and ....Why?" she asked. "Why do you ask?"

"I want it," he said.

She turned to face him quickly. "Honey—"

"I want it," he said quietly. "Now."

"But—"

"There are two of you," he said. "You and Bob. And Bob's a doctor, and head wounds are tricky things, and I wouldn't want Larry Wilson to have a relapse now and die, convenient as it might be for you and Bob."

She looked at him oddly. There was in her attitude none of the anger he had expected; he had thought she would be furious and shrill, but he had misjudged her. Instead of indignation, she showed him nothing at all except a faint pallor and a certain tightness about the mouth; for a moment he even had the thought that he had hurt her and she was going to start to cry, but she did not. She merely turned on her heel and walked out of the room. In less than a minute she was back. She put on the coverlet a nickel-plated weapon with pearl grips, and a box of cartridges marked *.320 ACP, for Automatic Colt*

Pistol. She did not speak. He checked the clip, which was full, and the cartridge in the chamber, and the safety, and put the gun under his pillow. The box of shells, more than three quarters full, he put into the drawer of the bedside table.

"Thank you, Elizabeth," he said gravely.

"Why, you're welcome, honey," she said in a small, stiff voice. "I declare, there's no reason why you should trust—us. I don't blame you a bit for being careful."

She turned abruptly away, but not before he had seen the tears in her eyes.

"Elizabeth—"

"What is it?" she demanded without looking around.

"Elizabeth, I'm sorry."

"I reckon there's no reason why you should be, honey. I—I'm a murderess. I've shot one man, my own husband. You can't t-take any chances. It m-might get to b-be a—a habit.... Heavens, I wish I wasn't all the time weeping!" she gasped, drawing her sleeve across her eyes; then she pretended abrupt interest in the wet smudges on the gold satin, which seemed to remind her of something, and she turned to examine her reflection in the mirror, lifting her hands to her head. "Honey, what's wrong with my hair, anyway?" she demanded, changing the subject brightly. "What was the old hen driving at? I think it looks real nice; it just needs to be set a little, that's all. What's the matter with it?"

"Why, nothing," Young said uncomfortably. Then it occurred to him that there was no good reason why he should not continue to be completely frank with this girl, after going so far as to demonstrate that he did not trust her. "Nothing," he said deliberately, "if you don't mind looking like a tramp."

Shocked, she swung about to face him. "Honey," she said in a dangerous voice, "honey, don't you start sniping at me, too! I got enough of that from my *real* husband and his darn old family to last me—If they had just let me alone; if they hadn't always acted as if they were sure I was going to disgrace the whole stupid tribe—" She checked herself abruptly, and turned back to the mirror, and passed her hand beneath the hair at the nape of her neck. When she spoke, her voice was flat and expressionless. "It's too long?"

He said, extremely embarrassed now, "Elizabeth, I'm no judge—"

"Honey, for heaven's sake!" she breathed. "You've just called me a murderess and a tramp. You're afraid I'm going to poison your soup and you're ashamed of the way I look, on top of it. Don't start getting coy now, hear?"

"It's too long," he said. "Either cut it off or put it up in some way."

"It's funny," she said softly. "I can remember Ma telling me that when she was young the real wild girls in town were the first to cut their hair off. Now you're a tart if you wear it too long....Anything else?"

"What?"

"Anything else you'd like to criticize, while you're in the mood?" Her voice was low and taut.

He hesitated, but there was no sense in holding back, now that he had started. "Sure," he said. "Your fingernails."

"What's the matter with them?" she demanded, glancing down. "They're clean, aren't they? Oh, you mean this old polish....I reckon you think this negligee's pretty crummy, too, and the house is a mess....I declare, the way a man can sit around in last week's pajamas with an inch of beard on his face and call a girl sloppy because she's got a spot on her dressing-gown! Honey—" Her voice ran out abruptly. She drew a long breath, like a sigh, and looked at herself in a mirror with an expression of distaste. "Honey," she said softly, "take me with you."

He did not realize at once what she had said, since she had seemed to be talking more to herself than to him. Then he looked at her quickly, and watched her come toward him. To his dismay, she went to her knees beside the bed, taking his hand in hers.

"Take me with you, David," she said. "I shouldn't ever have come here. Take me out of here. Please!"

"But—"

"You'll need me," she whispered. "We'll be Mr. and Mrs. Wilson, hear? We'll go—somewhere. Nobody will think anything of it, except the Decker girl, and what can she do except get mad? I'll just be taking you away somewhere to convalesce from your accident. It'll look just as if we'd made up and gone away on a second honeymoon, kind of; as if I'd forgiven you for last summer and taken you back, as if you'd changed your mind and decided you hadn't made such a bad mistake after all, family or no family."

He said, "Elizabeth—"

Then she was on her feet again, making the awkward movements of rising seem easy and graceful; and her voice was prosaic when she spoke:

"Think it over, honey. There's also the money; it's a joint account and I've still got his power of attorney that he made out for me once when they were sending him to the Pacific for something or other to do with ships."

Young said, "I wouldn't touch a cent of that bastard's—"

Elizabeth smiled. "Now you're being silly. You've taken his name and his home, you've been eating his food; you've kissed his wife. Why get high-minded about the money? It's—it's no good to him any longer, is it?"

Young looked at her; and she waited. The soft but direct light from the open window made her look young and expectant and quite lovely. As you got to know a girl, Young reflected, the details that had first jarred on you no longer seemed very important. It occurred to him, rather shockingly, that he now knew this girl better than he knew any other person in the world. He knew her fears and he could guess at her ambitions; he knew how to make her laugh and how to make her cry. She probably knew as much about him. By accident she had found her way closer to him than anybody had managed in a long time; even though he did not fully trust her, she was the one person in years that he had felt free to talk to.

You could put it nicely, he thought, and say that they seemed to get along well together because they suited each other; or you could make it ugly and say that they damn well had better get along because they knew too much about each other not to. Either way, they got along, and he knew suddenly that they always would, because neither of them would ever expect too much of the other. They would always make allowances. Both of them knew that there was not a great deal to expect. Between them was the unspoken understanding that they were both second-rate people who, in some important respects, had failed themselves.

They made a nice pair, Young thought grimly: a

pretty, somewhat shopworn young wife turned murderess and a big, somewhat beat-up young Naval officer turned— He did not finish the sentence, pushing the ugly word back into the darkness out of which it had come. He looked at the girl standing above him, and thought, *Why not?*

"Hell," he said, "It's a deal."

She nodded, and said in a practical voice, "Don't say anything to Bob when he comes. He—wouldn't understand."

Young thought that this was very likely; and he was wryly amused to discover that, now that he had committed himself, the thought of Bob Henshaw—bald and middle-aged though he might be—gave him a pang of jealousy. Elizabeth flushed a little under his regard. Suddenly he was aware of a warm feeling of sympathy for her, and he thought, *Poor kid, she must have been lonely as hell here, to take up with that old goat.* The thought of going away with her began to take shape in his mind, not unpleasantly.

He said, looking up at her, "You don't know what I look like. You've never seen my face."

"I'll like it," she said. "If I don't, I can always—close my eyes, like this." Smiling, she bent down and kissed him full on the mouth.

Chapter Eight

The screaming annoyed him. Here he was risking his damn life, working his fool head off with the ship likely to go any minute now, and he had to listen to that! So the guy was hurt; who wasn't? Did he want to get out or didn't he? What the devil was *he* expected to do about it, knock off for five minutes to sympathize? He was doing his goddamn best; the bastard might at least have the decency to appreciate it and keep his goddamn big mouth shut.... Then he was in the water, as it always happened, with fuel oil in his mouth and his hands hurting like nothing had any business to hurt. The great blazing hulk of the carrier drifted down on him inexorably in the moments before, jolted and rocked and shattered by a fresh series of explosions, she rolled over and went down stern first.

But the screaming continued still, a nasty, breathless, whimpering noise now. It seemed to come from a long way off, and he listened to it, still angered by it, for what seemed like a long time before he understood that he was making it. He fought his way upward through heavy layers of sleep and took control of himself and stopped it.

He lay afterward, wet with perspiration, waiting for the pounding of his heart to subside. Then the ceiling light came on above him, without warning, shockingly bright. He had opened his eyes instinctively at the click, and so looked directly into the sudden blaze of illumination; in the moment of blindness that followed he was aware of someone rushing toward the bed. The thought of the pistol under the pillow crossed his mind as he shoved himself up; but before he could reach for it, she was crouching beside him, touching him, clearly identified and no danger.

"Honey," she gasped, "honey, what's the matter, what happened?"

"I'm sorry, Elizabeth," he said, embarrassed at having awakened her at this hour and in such fashion. "I just had a nightmare. It's a bad habit of mine." He managed to laugh. "You just don't know what you're letting yourself in for—" Then he checked himself, because she was no longer looking at him. She had sunk down to kneel beside the bed with her head on her folded arms; and her breath was coming in great sobs. "Elizabeth!" he said, startled.

He regarded her with concern and remorse. He could think of nothing to do about it, however, but caress her hair gently as she knelt there beside him, her body shaken by the ragged violence of her breathing. Presently she stirred under his touch and, as if sensing the nature of his thoughts, gave a minute shake of her head without looking up.

"Honey, I'm all right…not crying…just all out of breath from running up that darn—those darn stairs!"

He could not help laughing at this anticlimax; yet it was still pleasant to know that there was somebody in the world who cared enough to come running when he made a fool of himself in the middle of the night. He glanced at the electric clock on the dresser, which read one-fifteen.

"What were you doing downstairs at this time of night, anyway?"

It was an idle question; but she was suddenly quite still and tense under his hand, so that touching her became suddenly awkward, and he took the hand away.

"Why," she said, her face still hidden and her voice muffled, "why, I—I couldn't sleep, honey. I went down to—" She paused, and went on quickly: "—to get a drink. I forgot to get a prescription from Bob and I'm all out of the pills. Sometimes a stiff drink—"

Her voice trailed off unconvincingly. A little time passed in silence. At last he reached over and tilted her face up to the harsh overhead light. Her eyes would not meet his. He looked at her, noting for the first time how she was dressed: in pale pink slacks of some kind of quite thin gabardine material and a pink nylon sweater with short sleeves. There was a single strand of pearls at her throat, he saw, and the soles of her sandals, visible as she knelt there, were damp.

She grew restless under his gaze and made a quick, furtive attempt, with one knee, to shove something out of sight beneath the bed, without looking down. He leaned over and picked up the object: a long, five-cell flashlight.

"I—I was outside," Elizabeth said.

"Uhuh."

"Don't look at me like that, honey," she whispered. "I can't bear to have you look at me like that."

She was making much more of a scene of it than it had seemed at first to deserve; the knowledge frightened him. He said harshly, "At least play it straight, sweetheart. Don't phony it up. You can't tell how I'm looking at you, with these damn bandages.

"Oh, you fool!" she cried. "Bandages! Do you think I can't tell from your eyes what—" Her voice failed again. "I didn't want you to know," she whispered presently. "That's why I lied."

"It's a fairly common reason for lying."

"I—I heard a noise," she said.

"Sure, you heard a burglar in the kitchen, so you got all dressed—"

"It was a boat," she said.

"A boat?" He did not understand at once.

"Out there." She indicated the window with a movement of her head. "I didn't want you to know because—because I was afraid you'd want to do something about it. I was curious, so I got dressed and sneaked down to look. Then you started to scream. I thought—I was afraid somebody had got into the house. I ran all the way up the hill from the beach; and you try doing that some night in the dark! Look at my slacks!" She showed him a knee dirtied by a fall. "I thought somebody was killing you, or something! I declare, it really worried me. Heaven knows why!"

He looked at her for a moment longer, oblivious to her resentment, not really seeing her now. "A boat," he said softly, and pulled back the covers to get out of bed.

"Honey," she said, "honey, it doesn't necessarily mean it's the one.... There are always boats anchoring in the cove. Why, it's a favorite spot; all the yachtsmen around here know it. It doesn't have to be the one Larry—"

Young swung his feet to the floor. "Could you read the name?"

"No. It was too dark."

"It is still there?"

"I suppose so, honey. They came ashore. There's a kind of public beach and launching place in there where you can drive a trailer down to the water; a strip of county land between our property and the Merediths', up the river. Their dinghy's still there, as far as I know. I was on my way over to look at it when.... You don't believe I'm telling you the truth, do you, David?"

It had not occurred to him to doubt her further. Now he looked at her sharply, disturbed by the question; but there was no time to waste in determining what lay behind it. He went quickly to the closet and found an old dressing gown of Larry Wilson's, and a pair of battered loafer shoes that were a little too small. He spoke over his shoulder.

"Did anybody meet them?"

"I didn't see anybody," she said. "I just woke up suddenly like you do and heard them rowing ashore. It seemed kind of late for anybody to be rowing, so I got up and looked. I saw the boat in the cove, and the dinghy. They pulled it up on the sand and walked up the road—"

"How many of them?"

"Two. Don't ask me to describe them, honey. I haven't the tiniest idea, what they look like—"

She checked herself abruptly. In the silence, the faint click and creak of rowlocks came clearly into the room. Young stepped quickly toward the window, but realized that the light in the room would silhouette him clearly for anyone on the river to see; he turned toward the switch, and knew that this would not do, either: the sudden darkening of what was probably the only lighted room in the house would be enough to alert any watcher.

He moved swiftly out into the hall and through the next door on the same side, finding himself in a room which, even in the dark, gave an impression of extreme femininity and utter untidiness. As he felt his way toward the window, he had a brief stifling sensation of pushing his way through a spider web of discarded, intimate, fragile garments; they hung from the doorknob and from the door itself, every article of furniture he touched seemed to be littered with them; he could even feel them underfoot. There was a confusing odor of cosmetics both fresh and stale. He reached the window and looked out, aware of Elizabeth beside him.

It was a clear night outside, with enough light for him to make out the graveled drive, a dim circle against the dark grass of the lawn, that reached to the still darker trees and bushes of the hillside. Over and through the trees, the river had a sheen like polished metal. A lighted window in a cottage on the far bank cast a long, almost unwavering reflection across the water. Closer, a yellow anchor light burned near the masthead of the small power cruiser in the cove. Somehow, the light was a letdown. It seemed unlikely that people on a secret and unlawful mission would announce their presence by burning the lights required by the rules of the road at sea, any more than a fleeing bank robber would let himself be delayed by an unfavorable traffic signal.

Young whispered, "Elizabeth, did your husband have any night glasses around the place? Binoculars, telescope, anything?"

She hesitated. "I don't think so, honey. If he had any, they'd be down on the *Amberjack*, wouldn't they?"

"Damn it, if I could just read the name—!"

As he watched, the riding light shifted through a brief arc as the little yacht rolled minutely to the weight of a person climbing aboard. Young heard the distant clatter of oars being stowed, the rattle of oarlocks being removed from their sockets, and the yacht rolled briefly again as a second person joined the first aboard. He could see the little white dinghy now, drifting back on the tide to lie astern; but the canopy over the larger craft's cockpit cast an impenetrable shadow, and be could not make out what the people aboard were doing.

Suddenly a shadowy form appeared forward, and at the same time the motor started, with a sputtering, liquid noise that was due to the exhaust's being located at the water line. The small figure on the forward deck, braced to the strain, brought the cable in hand over hand, paused for a moment as the anchor came awash, sloshing it back and forth to clean the mud from it; then the hook was aboard and the yacht was moving ahead. The riding light went out smartly and the running lights came on; coming to cruising speed, the craft made a wide turn to pick up the channel outside the cove, and faded into the darkness to the southeast. Presently the wake made a belated, rhythmic, rushing sound along the shore.

"Well—" Young said, and let his voice die. There was nothing to say. A boat had come in, its crew had gone ashore to stretch their legs; they had returned aboard; they had taken their little ship out again. They had been careful to break no regulation regarding the handling of small craft in the navigable inland waters of the United States; they were probably even thoughtful enough not to dump the garbage or flush the head until they were well offshore. There was no law that said yachtsmen could not step ashore for a taste of terra firma at one o'clock in the morning.

Chapter Nine

Elizabeth spoke quietly: "Can I turn on a light now?"

"Sure," he said. "Sure."

"I declare," she said, "I don't know if I ought to. The room's such a mess."

But the light came on anyway, and he turned to look at her. She faced him, he thought, a little defiantly, as if awaiting his anger; although he knew of no good reason why he should be angry with her. He certainly hoped she did not think he still held her little deceit against her. Yet there was a kind of pleading in the way she took a step forward now, almost shyly, in the manner of a pretty girl who wants to be forgiven for something. He hesitated, troubled and uneasy; then drew her to him and held her with an emotion that was curiously compounded of affection and desire and grief, the last because he wanted very much to trust her but knew that he could not afford to, and perhaps never would. Not that it made a great difference. Theirs was not a relationship built upon trust and respect but simply upon loneliness and mutual need.

Presently, still holding her, he said, "Don't you ever pick up in here, sweetheart? God, what a rat's nest! Where was you brought up, in a barn?"

She poked him very lightly in the chest, just enough to make it clear that she could have hurt him had she wanted to. "Never you mind where I was brought up, hear? Get back to your own room if—if you don't like it here."

There was silence between them for a while. Then she raised her head to look up at him, and he looked down at her, conscious as never before of the shape of her face and the delicately wanton curve of her mouth. The thin slacks and sweater showed her figure in a new and pleasant light. Some girls looked slim and boyish in pants; it was a nice way for them to look, but it was not particularly exciting. But there was nothing boyish about Elizabeth's looks, although she was slim enough. The slacks seemed to emphasize the feminine smallness of her waist and the graceful roundness of her hips. The light sweater made it almost embarrassingly clear that she was wearing nothing beneath it. An impulse that he could not resist made him lift a hand to confirm this impression gently, uneasily aware that the bandages made him an unromantic and perhaps even repulsive figure; he was fully prepared for her to strike his hand away, but she caught it with her own and held it to her breast for a moment.

"David," she whispered. "Honey—"

Then she was lying against him hard, and her mouth was urgent and possessive against his; and he was no longer aware of himself or his surrounding, only of her. Despite the clothes she was wearing there was no awkwardness or embarrassment in what followed: the small delay—and her breathless laughter at his clumsiness—only served to make more complete the ultimate fulfillment.

Afterward they lay on the bed for a while, silent, in each other's arms. She was the first to speak.

"David—"

"Yes."

"Honey, you're breaking my arm."

He laughed at this, and moved to let her free herself. He was surprised to find that there was still light in the room; there had been a space of time when light and darkness had meant nothing. The light did not disturb him; there could no longer be any question of modesty between them, and he was pleased to be able to see her face. He pushed the dark hair back from her forehead gently, lying beside her on the bed. Regarding her, he could not help wondering what might be in store for them together; the present was pleasant enough but the future looked unpromising, to say the least. The same thought must have come to her, because the smile with which she had been watching him died.

"Honey," she whispered, "honey, let's get out of here."

"Now?"

"Yes, now." Her voice became stronger. "I have money. I have about four thousand dollars in the house—" She flushed a little as he looked at her sharply. "Well, I'm not *stupid,* honey! I declare, men sometimes act as if women had no sense at all. After—after what happened, it seemed like I might need some money in a hurry, so—so I got some, and not out of the local bank, either. Out of one of his New York accounts where it won't show up for a while. We can go a long way on four thousand dollars, and nobody knows he's dead. You can just keep on being Larry Wilson—some place where nobody will know the difference even after you get those bandages off—and I can be taking care of your affairs for you while you recover from your accident." She sat up quickly. "Honey, come on!"

He hesitated, with an odd feeling of reluctance, as if leaving this house with her would be the final step in the process of degeneration that had started when he had first refrained from establishing his identity at the hospital.

"What about Henshaw?" he asked.

"Oh, Bob will just have to take care of himself," she said carelessly. It seemed like a cavalier way for her to dismiss the older man, who had, after all, risked a great deal for her. Young watched her get up and climb into her slacks, an action that not even she could make look graceful. She jerked the fastener closed and turned to look at him. "Well?"

Her impatience was contagious. Certainly he had no desire to remain in this place, but he hadn't forgotten Henshaw's threat either. "Well, all right," he said hesitantly. "All right, Elizabeth."

Later, he never remembered a great deal about the half hour that followed, perhaps because he was weaker than he had realized until he started back to his room to get dressed. He remembered that she had to pick out the clothes for him and help him put them on. He remembered that it became funny, and that both of them laughed crazily at the startling picture he made when she placed one of Larry Wilson's discarded hats upon his bandaged head. He remembered that the house already had a deserted and shut-up look when they came down the stairs. She had already packed the bags and brought them down—they were standing by the door—and the lights had been turned out; only the hall light was burning. He remembered that he was carrying the flashlight because she would have to manage the bags, and that this embarrassed him a little, in a masculine way.

He stopped in the small hallway between the stairs and the front door to catch his breath for the descent.

It occurred to him that he had never been downstairs in this house before, to be aware of it; and he looked about him curiously, finding himself between the dining room, to the right, and the living room, to the left. On the living room table, within his range of vision, an incongruous object gleamed dully in the light that spilled through the archway that separated this room from the hall.

"Honey, come *on!*" Elizabeth said impatiently, but he pulled himself free and moved forward to look at the large and efficient-looking binoculars lying on the mahogany table that was badly in need of dusting. They were Navy 7x50's, a type with which he was quite familiar. He remembered that they made pretty good night glasses; and he remembered something else, and turned to look at the girl who had come into the room behind him.

The light was behind her, but he could read the defiance in her attitude. "All right," she said. "All right, I lied about them. I didn't want you looking at that boat with binoculars, honey. You've got such a funny conscience."

Young said, "But you looked at it." She nodded, and he asked, "What was the name?"

She licked her lips and hesitated. She spoke almost sullenly: "Well, they're gone, so it doesn't matter now, does it?"

"Tell me."

She said, "Honey, what difference does it make? You can't do anything about it, can you?" She made a quick gesture, as he stepped forward. "Honey, keep your shirt on! It was a funny name. I'm trying to remember....*Marbeth,*" she said triumphantly. "That's it. *Marbeth, New York.*"

He looked down at her shadowed face. The list she had taken from him was still clear in his mind: *Shooting Star, Aloha, Marbeth*....She caught his arm as he moved.

"David, what are you going to do?"

The question stopped him. He could think of nothing to do that would not bring complete disaster down upon both of them; and on the other hand, what did he know? A man who was dead had carried a list of boats, which had been destroyed. One of these boats had showed up, presumably to meet the man; not finding him, it had departed. There was a presumption of illegal and perhaps even treasonous activities, but it was only a presumption, based upon Larry Wilson's reputation. There was no proof at all.

Elizabeth gripped his arm tightly. "Come on, honey," she said. "We're wasting time. It's none of our business, is it?" She kissed him quickly. "We can be a long ways from here by morning if we hurry, hear? Don't forget the flashlight."

He found himself wishing desperately to be well and strong again; he seemed incapable of seeing the alternatives clearly. He let her urge him toward the door. She released him to pick up the bags and follow him.

"Honey," she said, "be careful. Did you bring the gun?"

He looked around sharply, surprised by the question. "What do you mean?"

She said, "Why, nothing. I mean, that boat. I declare, I'm just all upset and nervous."

He studied her for a moment, noting that her eyes were not quite candid. He remembered the dampness of her sandals: she had been outside, earlier in the evening. He drew a deep breath and patted his pocket to reassure himself about the presence of the gun. He opened the door, which opened inward, so that he had to step back a pace. An utterly familiar voice whispered from the darkness outside.

"Well, did you finally get your patient to sleep, Elizabeth? I must say it took you long enough! I've been wait—"

Young was not aware of pressing the switch, but the flashlight beam shot out across the lawn and swung in the direction from which the whisper had come. Then the night seemed to erupt with a bellowing noise: the sound of a heavy revolver fired at close range. Something smashed the flashlight from Young's hand, not only taking it away from him but demolishing it in the process, and numbing his arm to the shoulder. There seemed to be an endless shower of broken glass and burst metal.

He was not aware of ducking, but he was on his knees in the doorway. The fall had wrenched his chest, and the agony of it joined with the stinging pain of his arm. A man was running away from him across the lawn; a big man with a revolver in one hand; a man wearing a light hat and topcoat that looked horribly familiar; and after a while he realized what was so horrible about it: the man he was looking at, who had just shot a flashlight out of his hand, was a man who was dead and buried, sunk in the Bay securely wrapped in fathoms of heavy chain....

Chapter Ten

Wakefulness came upon him suddenly and he sat up, finding himself on a sofa in a living room gray with daylight. He sat there for a moment, bewildered; then he caught sight of his right wrist decorated with a large, fresh, Band-Aid.

It came back to him then: the flashlight shattering in his hand and the figure running across the lawn, and he thought, *He's alive. The bastard's alive!* The thought left him with a curious mixture of exultation and panic.

He could remember Elizabeth helping him in here afterward; the shock seemed to have taken his remaining strength. Neither of them had said anything; there had been nothing to say. The identity of that single figure running across the lawn in the darkness, gun in hand, had showed that her whole behavior from the beginning had almost certainly been one great calculated falsehood. *Almost?* Young thought grimly, *Why almost?* The husband she had claimed to have murdered was alive; her whole story had been a fabric of deceit.

He shook his head and looked about the living room, a long, high, noble room filled with furniture—too much furniture—that, except for the television set in the corner, had an old-American look to it. Young had no way of knowing if the stuff was genuine, never having paid much attention to antiques. He did notice the liquor rings, and the cigarette burns and dust. A spiral of smoke rose lazily from a cluttered ashtray on the floor by a big chair near the door. He watched it for a while, then rose and extinguished the smoldering butt. There was, he saw, a coffee cup and a plate with half a sandwich on the small table beside the chair. A motion-picture magazine with a torn cover lay open and face down, on the seat of the chair. On the arm of the chair lay the nickel-plated automatic pistol he had put into his pocket before leaving his room the night before.

He frowned at all of this, put the gun back into his pocket, and went out into the hall. The shattered flashlight was still lying to the right of the front door where the bullet had hurled it; little shards of glass from the lens were scattered glittering all over the floor. The two packed suitcases stood in the middle of the hall where Elizabeth had dropped them, after the shot, as she ran forward to help him. None of this had been touched since last night. Even the hall light was still burning.

He switched it off, picked up the broken flashlight, and went on through the dining room into the kitchen, which had apparently been modernized fairly recently. It was one of those bright laboratories of formica, rubber tile, and white enameled steel which the appliance companies liked to recommend as proper settings for their products. This one had the works, including an electric stove with the most elaborate instrument panel of Young's experience; it had a refrigerator, deep-freeze, dishwasher, and fluorescent lighting; it had a breakfast nook in one corner; and it was spotlessly clean. Elizabeth was standing at the stove, still wearing the pink slacks and sweater of the night before. She did not look around when he came through the swinging door.

"Breakfast will be ready in a minute," she said.

He asked, "What do I do with this?"

The question forced her to glance over her shoulder at the flashlight he held out. He saw that her face had the pale and shiny look of sleeplessness.

"Heavens, throw it anywhere," she said irritably. "Why ask me? There's a trash can somewhere around."

"Thanks," he said. "And where do I find a broom?"

"What?"

"A broom. To sweep the glass out of the front hall, or do you think it adds to the quaint charm of the place?"

She ignored his sarcasm. "There's a broom in the broom closet."

He checked the obvious retort, located the closet in question and equipped himself, and started out of the kitchen. At the door he stopped.

"Why the gun?"

She poked at the sputtering contents of the skillet, and pushed at her hair with the back of the hand that held the spatula, before turning to look at him again. "What, honey?"

"The gun. Last known to be reposing in my pants pocket, this morning discovered on the living room easychair."

"Why," she said, "I was scared he might come back."

"So you stood watch all night? Thanks."

"I'm not asking you to believe it, honey."

"I didn't say I didn't believe it."

"I declare, it's pretty obvious what you think. Well, go do your sweeping, hear? These eggs won't wait forever."

When he returned, she was setting two places in the breakfast nook. He put the broom away where he had found it and paused by the adjacent window to look out. There was a low fog on the river, just dissipating in the sunlight, and a white sloop, sails furled, was gliding down the channel with the magical look of a sailboat proceeding through a flat calm under auxiliary power.

The masthead remained in sight at all times, but the lower rigging and the hull kept losing themselves in the mist.

Young said, "Well, she's right on schedule."

"Who?"

"The Decker kid."

"Oh."

The sloop slid past the dock and the big power cruiser moored there, and swung away out of the mist, toward open water. Young watched it for a while, with uneasy speculation. The small figure slouched in the cockpit looked harmless enough at this distance; she was wearing a short, bright green jacket and a matching hat that hid the color of her hair. She appeared to be smoking a cigarette; presently she rose and pitched the butt over the side and went below, leaving her ship to shift for itself. After a while the little vessel began to swing off course. The girl came out of the cabin carrying what seemed to be a mug of coffee, glanced casually around, and remedied the situation. Then she stood there, facing forward, drinking her coffee and steering with the tiller between her bare knees, with a kind of negligent and arrogant confidence. Confident people annoyed Young, and he looked away, to find Elizabeth beside him.

"What is it, honey?"

"Nothing," he said. "I wish I knew how the kid fits

into this." Then he shrugged his shoulders. "That's a lot to ask. Hell, I don't even know how I fit into it, do I, Elizabeth?"

"David," she said. "Honey—"

He swung away from her. "What's that cruiser doing down there, anyway?" he asked abruptly. "It couldn't have wintered there; even if you don't have enough ice here to cut it to pieces one good storm would have finished it. It's a hell of an exposed location to keep a boat tied up to a dock, even in summer."

She said, "Why, Larry used to— Does it matter, honey?"

"I'm asking," he said.

She sighed. "All right. Larry used to keep it at a mooring you had to row out to, but before he left he took the boat to the yard and pulled the mooring up on shore. This spring I—I got a letter from him asking me to have the yard fix it up and bring it around; it—seemed like little enough to do."

He did not look at her. He knew her well enough now that he did not even have to see her face to know when she was lying, although her reasons were not always clear.

"I declare," she said, "I didn't know I was going to have to look after it like a baby or I'd never— Bob had to show me how to pump out the water and fix the ropes and the bumpers or whatever you call them...." Her voice died away. "Breakfast is ready, honey," she said at last.

He nodded, not trusting himself to look at her. He held tightly to the thought of the gun, heavy in his pocket. Liar or not, she had sat up all night with a gun to protect him as he slept. He wanted to believe that.

There was an uncomfortable intimacy to the breakfast nook in the corner; it was hard to retain an attitude of aloofness toward a girl when you had to face her in a cramped space where your knees met, across a tiny table over which your hands were bound to collide in reaching for one thing or another for which neither of you had wanted to ask, not wanting to accept any favors or assistance whatever. After a while the silence became ridiculous, and Young spoke.

"This is a nice kitchen you've got here."

"At least it's mine," she said without raising her glance from the plate.

"What do you mean?"

"All the rest is his or his family's. This is mine." Her voice became stronger. "I declare, I never thought I'd settle for a darn old kitchen, but—but it's the only place in the house where I can sit and look at something that never belonged to anybody else, just me. Just me and Westinghouse and General Electric, honey." She licked her lips. "That stove—that stove didn't come out of the country house of Colonel Oglethorpe Wilson's maternal grandmother. It just came straight from Mr. Spofford, the local dealer, to me. The deep-freeze—the deep-freeze wasn't ever a part of the estate of—of Governor Winthrop Wilson and nobody ever had to trace it to the attic of a little old farm down in the south end of the county and—have it restored by— I don't have to remember where the darn thing came from, either, or why it's important. It's important because it keeps the food cold, and if it doesn't work I send for a serviceman, and if it wears out I'll get rid of it and buy another one. I—I don't have to pretend I think it's something precious and wonderful just because it once belonged to some old fogy I never saw who'd have looked down his nose at me like all the rest of the stupid, pompous, stuck-up—"

She checked herself abruptly, and drew a long, harsh breath. After a moment she made as if to rise. He pulled his knees out of the way, and she slid out of the booth and walked quickly to the stove. He saw her use a knuckle at the corner of one eye, before she picked up the coffee pot and came back to fill the cups. Then she carried the pot back to the stove and stood there for a moment. The way her shoulders squared themselves slightly beneath the thin, pink sweater, before she turned again, told him that she had made up her mind, at last, to speak.

"Honey," she said, "honey, I didn't know it was going to be like this. I didn't know it was going to be you."

Then she walked quickly toward the door, almost running before she got there; but when she reached the door she stopped and turned again.

"And I—I didn't know he was going to be there last night; and I didn't know he even had a gun. You mustn't think— I can't bear it if you think— I didn't send you out that door to be shot at; I didn't!"

When he reached her, she had turned her face against the door jamb, pressing against it hard as if seeking the pain, so that when she looked up at him, sensing him above her, there was a small, round, pink mark in the center of her forehead. He noticed that there was a trace of dried blood on her cheek; presumably where a flying sliver of glass had cut her the night before. This disturbed him; he took out his handkerchief and moistened it with his tongue and wiped the blood away gently, relieved to find that the cut itself was insignificant. All this time she was watching him with wide, questioning eyes. The pink mark on her forehead had died away again, so that her face was quite pale, even to the lips. Suddenly she was in his arms.

After a while he said, "Elizabeth."

Her voice was muffled. "Yes, honey."

"Pardon me," he said, stroking her hair, "but isn't it

about time to decide whose team you're pitching for?" He felt her become quite still. "I love you but I can't take a hell of a lot more of this; and I don't think you can, either. You've got to make up your mind; you can't have it both ways. First, you protect Larry Wilson from me and then you turn around and sit up all night to protect me from Larry Wilson and then you turn around again and start lying like hell to protect him.... It won't work, darling. I mean, you can't have it both ways, or did I say that? I appreciate that the guy is your husband and that there are some things you can't do to anybody you've once been married to. Even the law doesn't demand that. I certainly don't ask it. But I'm conceited enough to think that you like me—"

He stopped, because her shoulders had begun to shake. He released her, startled, and saw her take a step backward and toss back her long, dark hair, with a swing of her head, to stare at him. Her hands came together to grip each other so tightly that the knuckles showed white and bloodless. Then her head went back and she was laughing helplessly, unable to stop.

Chapter Eleven

He spoke into the telephone. "This is Lawrence Wilson. Yes, Wilson. I'd like to speak to Dr. Henshaw, please.... Doc, you'd better get out here on the double. Elizabeth's throwing some kind of a wingding and I'll be damned if I can get her to snap out of.... All right, Doc."

He put the phone down, drew a long breath, and went back up the stairs to the big light room with its basically neat, old-fashioned furniture that was overlaid, as if with tidal debris, with the litter of Elizabeth's occupancy. She looked a little like tidal debris herself, lying where she had flung herself across the big, untidy bed. She had a pillow pressed to her face and he thought she had stuffed part of it into her mouth to silence herself. Her body had a look of trembling rigidity like that, he thought, of a hawser stretched to the breaking point; when a line began to vibrate like that you slacked off quickly if you did not want it to carry away.

But there was nothing he could do. He had considered slapping her face—a popular remedy—and had found himself incapable of striking her. He had also debated putting her into the bathtub and turning on the cold shower, but this had seemed like a messy and humiliating procedure, especially if it did not work. Besides, the sight of him, or his touch, seemed to set her off again; and although he was tremendously worried about her he could not help resenting, a little, being considered so excruciatingly funny, even by a girl who at the moment was obviously not responsible for her own behavior.

It was a relief to hear the car in the drive. Young stepped out of the room as silently as he had entered, and waited by the stairs. Presently the doctor's bald head appeared, and Henshaw came up, somewhat breathless from the climb, carrying his bag. He passed Young with a nodded greeting, went to the bedroom door and looked in, and turned back again.

"What happened, Mr. Young?"

"We had a kind of rough night out here, Doc," Young said. He had had time to think things over; and now he studied the man facing him with some care. Henshaw looked as middle-aged and respectable as ever in the same or another baggy brown suit: a heavy, sagging man with a lined, honest face, the mouth of which, however, had a slightly peevish and womanly look. Young had not noticed that look before, but he noticed it now. A man with a mouth like that was not to be trusted. "Kind of rough,"

Young said softly. "I guess it just got her down. I almost threw one myself when it happened. I've been shot at by a lot of people, mostly Japs, but I've never had a ghost use me as a target before."

Something changed in Henshaw's eyes. "A ghost?"

"Let's quit kidding, Doc," Young said gently. "I don't know what's going on around here, but I do know that Larry Wilson's alive. He took a potshot at me last night. Elizabeth put me to bed and stayed up with a gun in case he should come back. Maybe it just wore her down, or maybe it was a delayed reaction or something; anyway, she got hysterical right after breakfast. I don't know just what set her off."

"Alive?" the doctor whispered. "Wilson is alive?"

Young said, "Cut it out, Doc. It was a good gag while it lasted, but now you can cut it out."

Henshaw let his breath go out in a little sigh. "All right, Mr. Young. I'll cut it out. We'll talk about it later." He took a fresh grip on his bag.

Young said, "Doc."

About to turn away, the older man looked back. "Yes?"

"Careful, Doc. Easy with the hypo. I suppose you have to put her to sleep, but it would be nice if she woke up again, don't you think?" Henshaw did not speak, and Young went on: "There's a lot of funny stuff going on around here, Doc, and you're one of the funnier parts, I think. Any man who goes for a woman half his age is a screwball anyway; and any doctor who'll monkey with murder, real or phony, doesn't really take his profession too damn seriously."

Henshaw licked his lips. His voice was somewhat shrill when he spoke. "You're hardly in a position to criticize anybody else's professional conduct—"

"Take it easy, Doc."

"I have told you: I do not like to be called Doc!"

"Don't get mad, Doc," Young said softly. "I'm just trying to make sure we understand each other, Doc."

Henshaw again moistened his lips with his tongue. "I—I understand," he said shakily. "You're doing me an injustice, but—I understand. I'll be careful."

Young stepped back, and watched the doctor go into the room and pull the door shut. He stood there for a moment longer and a sentence from the conversation drifted unwanted through his mind: *You're hardly in a position to criticize anybody else's professional conduct.* Young shivered, took his hand from the gun in his pocket, finding it sweaty, and turned away.

From his own room—the room he had come to think of as his—he could hear the voices next door, Elizabeth's high and breathless at first, gradually becoming calmer. The thick walls of the old house prevented him from making out what she was saying. Presently the voices died away, the door opened, and he heard Henshaw come along the hall.

The doctor entered the room and set his bag on the dresser. "Now you, Mr. Young," he said.

"Never mind me," Young said. "I'm doing fine. How is she?"

"She will be all right when she wakes up."

"And when will that be?"

"Two or three hours, perhaps longer since you indicated that she did not get much sleep last night."

"Let's take a look," Young said.

Henshaw shrugged and together they moved quietly into Elizabeth's room. The girl was lying peacefully in the bed. Her breathing seemed deep and even. Her face was pale, but not as pale as it had been; she was never, Young reminded himself, a really robust-looking girl. He was helplessly aware that she could be dying before his eyes and he would not know it; and when he glanced at the man beside him he saw that Henshaw knew this too and was amused by it.

"She's all right, Mr. Young. I give you my word. I would not harm her."

Elizabeth stirred at the whisper and made a little sound and was still again. The two men glanced at each other guiltily and moved on tiptoe out of the room. Young closed the door gently. They did not speak again until they were downstairs.

Young cleared his throat. "How about some coffee? I never got to finish mine."

"All right, Mr. Young." When they were seated in the little booth in the kitchen, the doctor studied his companion for a moment and said, "You seem to have taken the bit in your teeth, Mr. Young. I don't suppose there's any harm in your being out of bed if you feel up to it, if you take things easy; but I advise you not to over-exert yourself for a while yet."

"All right, Doctor Henshaw."

The older man looked down into his coffee cup. "She was mine until you came," he said abruptly. "It was the most wonderful thing in my life, Mr. Young. I—I have never been very popular in that way; my family is a good one, as good as any around here, but there was never much money and I had to work very hard to get through medical school. For a not very brilliant man without financial support to get through medical school— The others had time for girls, but I did not. And the internship, and starting in practice, and building it up year after year, and then the war came along and I was sent out to the West Coast, where I was put to treating, not wounded soldiers, not even soldiers with colds and venereal disease, but their dependents! Sniveling children and complaining women for four years, free, while everything I had built here fell apart; and when I returned the younger doctors who had been overseas were already back and doing very well at the expense of the practice I used to have.... Well, I am making a living again, and I suppose I should not complain. Certainly I do not ask you to sympathize. I merely want you to understand what it meant to me that—that a girl like Elizabeth could even look at me. I just want you to know why—I did what I did. I have told Elizabeth. I think she understands. I do not expect her to forgive me."

Young said, "Can you blame her? But you might be wrong. She forgives easy."

"It no longer matters, does it?" Henshaw said. "I seem to have lost her anyway." There was silence between them for a while. At last the doctor looked up. "How much do you know, Mr. Young?"

Young moved his shoulders. "Enough, I think."

"I should like to hear your conclusions."

Young said, "Well, I was told a pretty complicated story when I arrived here. I was told that she had shot her husband and called you, and you had disposed of the body for her. When I saw him alive last night, naturally my first thought was that both of you had been lying. I figured you must both have been playing ball with him, keeping him hidden, feeding me this line of tripe to keep me quiet; she because he's her husband and you because—well, maybe he was blackmailing you, having caught you playing around with his wife. Something like that. That was my first idea."

"It was wrong," Henshaw said.

Young said, "That's right, it was wrong. Her hysterics put me on the right track. When I tried to figure out what hit her so hard this morning, Doc, I came on a funny thing. She'd been perfectly all right—a little tired and upset, but all right—until I mentioned Larry Wilson's name. Before that, we had both been talking about the guy who had shot at me, but we'd each been taking for granted that the other knew who it was. Yet she'd been a couple of steps behind me when the shot was fired, well back in the hall. I decided that she'd never seen the guy at all. She had thought it was somebody else entirely!"

Henshaw had started to drink from his cup; now he put it down again gently. "Who, Mr. Young?"

"Why, you, Doc," Young said. "She'd thought it was you. You see, we were about to run out on you. It probably bothered her; she probably felt guilty about leaving you, cold, like that. Suddenly a gun goes off in our faces, I'm lying there bleeding—a little, anyway—and somebody takes off across the lawn. Naturally Elizabeth jumped to the conclusion that it was you; that you'd suspected something, sneaked back to keep an eye on us, and lost your head when you saw us about to run away together. Why shouldn't she think that—*if she had no idea her husband was alive?*"

He looked across the table at the older man. Henshaw would not meet his eyes. Young stood up abruptly, pushed his way out of the booth, and took his coffee cup to the stove and refilled it.

"You're kind of a louse, aren't you, Doc?" he said softly, without looking around. "To let her go all this time thinking she was a murderer! It's no wonder she blew her top when I let slip it was Wilson who shot at me last night!"

Henshaw said, "I have told her I was sorry. I have tried to explain the circumstances—"

"Circumstances!" Young said.

"How did you guess?"

Young said, "Damn it, the person who shoots a man might make a mistake about his being dead. But the person who buries him can be damn sure!" He drew a long breath. "If Wilson was alive, that made you a liar, Doc. You never dumped him out in the Bay with a mooring chain about him. They don't get up out of six fathoms of water and come back to shoot off guns. He never went over the side at all, did he, Doc?"

He swung about, but Henshaw did not look up. The doctor studied the dregs of his coffee and said quietly, "I am, after all, a physician, and one always likes to check on a preliminary diagnosis before—taking any drastic action. You can imagine my emotions upon discovering that Larry was alive. The bullet had merely stunned him and caused him to lose some blood. Naturally, I couldn't—couldn't push a living man over—"

Young said, "Hell, there was no reason why you

should! But why in God's name didn't you come roaring back to tell her the good news?"

The doctor seemed to shrink a little at the question. Then he got up slowly, picked up his bag, and turned to face Young. "I was afraid," he said. "I—I have worked too hard and too long for—for what little position I have managed to attain. When I brought him back to consciousness he would not let me tell her, Mr. Young. He was very pleased with the knowledge that she thought him dead by her hand. He is a terrible, ruthless, and vengeful young man; he not only threatened me with scandal, as you suggested, but he promised to implicate me in his own dirty undercover game if I ever told anyone he was alive. And as you know, these days one hint of disloyalty can absolutely ruin the most respectable— The very fact that I was involved with his wife—I could not face it, Mr. Young. I simply could not face it, after all I have been through to get where I am. It may not seem like much to you, or to anybody else, but I have worked hard for it. . . ."

Chapter Twelve

He stood outside the front door watching Henshaw's coupé pull away, and he remained there for a while after the car had gone out of sight. It was a pleasant day, with a steadily freshening southeasterly breeze. One of the local fishing boats was running down along the opposite shore of the river, slipping through the water at surprising speed with very little fuss, a characteristic of these long and narrow hulls. Young watched it idly, feeling empty and planless. Presently Elizabeth would wake up and they would make another attempt to get away from this place, but he discovered that he had lost faith in the notion. He could not see them together anywhere but here....

A glint of light on the water well to one side and astern of the distant fisherman brought him out of this gloomy reverie. The sun had not yet swung around to this quadrant; there were glittering reflections out toward the estuary now, where the southeasterly breeze was kicking up a brisk chop in the path of the light, but there was no obvious cause for any bright glints at this point in midstream well up in the calmer waters of the river. Young considered the spot that had caught his eye with the half-focused attention he had learned at sea, not concentrating on the one point but ready to pick up anything distracting anywhere within his field of vision; so that when the phenomenon occurred again he was prepared for it. It was closer this time but still over half a mile away, just a brief disturbance in the water opposite the wooded point upstream where the river, narrowing, curved out of sight. It might have looked like the splash of a breaking wave or a rising fish—to anyone but a man who, some time ago when periscopes had been a matter of concern to a lot of people, had become very well acquainted with the behavior of waves and fishes.

Young walked quickly into the living room and picked up the binoculars that were still lying on the table there. He carried them back to the front door. It took him a minute to adjust the eyepieces for his vision; another minute passed before he could pick up the curious, recurring splash in the field of the lenses, much closer to shore now.

The range was still fairly long—he estimated nine hundred yards—and it was hard for him, weak and out of practice, to hold the heavy binoculars steady on the target. He braced himself against the door jamb and drew a long breath and held it; and so managed at last to get a good look at the small object—rhythmically appearing and almost disappearing—that was the head of a swimmer doing an inconspicuous breast stroke toward the point up the river.

As Young watched, the distant swimmer broke into a rapid crawl for half a dozen strokes and stood up abruptly in shoal water some distance from shore, standing there for a moment resting in the head-down, hands-on-knees attitude of the winded athlete. The range made recognition difficult, even through the glasses, but the light was good and he had no trouble distinguishing a green satin bathing suit that, while scanty enough, included one item more than a man would have found necessary. *Why, the damn little mermaid!* he said to himself silently. As he watched, the girl squeezed the short red hair back from her face and leaned sideways to pound the water out of one ear. Then she gave a quick uneasy glance in his direction, as if remembering that she was standing in plain sight of the distant house, and ran ashore and disappeared among the trees and tall grasses on the point.

Young lowered the glasses, nodding slowly to himself, although he could not have said why he did so. He glanced at his watch and looked around. The front step was certainly no place to wait, even sheltered by the screen. He did not think she could have spotted him with the unaided eye at the distance, but from now on the advantage would be all hers. She could make her approach from any direction.... Somehow he found himself quite certain that she would come here. When he had last seen her, she had been aboard her little sloop, heading out toward the Bay through the morning mist. She must have put in at some cove along the shore out of sight and made her way back here on foot to where she could swim the river; she had not gone to all that trouble just to get home. He wondered what had brought her back, but there was no way of knowing, or even guessing. The dining room was the best location from which to look out for her, he decided; from the corner windows there he could cover the upstream side and the front of the house without exposing himself. The other two sides would have to go unguarded; of course, it was not a matter of guarding the place from attack—one red-haired kid in a two-piece bathing suit could hardly constitute a real danger—but of observing what she was up to. He stationed himself in the corner by a large dark sideboard and glanced at his watch; three minutes had passed since she had disappeared. It would be a mile around the cove by the shortest route. He frowned, estimating what speed a barefooted girl could be expected to make through the woods. Two knots at best, he thought, give her half an hour. He settled down to wait.

It took somewhat less time than he had expected, because she was taking less care than he had thought she would. At eighteen minutes he caught sight of her again. She was three-quarters of the way around the cove, running openly along the beach down there. Perhaps she was counting on the trees to shield her from the house as she came below it, but they were not thick enough to keep Young from catching the flash of the green bathing suit, a shinier and more brilliant green than the foliage. He could follow her progress quite plainly despite the wire mesh of the window screen through which he was looking.

The kid was in good condition; running did not seem to bother her, even after her lengthy swim. She plugged right along the narrow bare strip beside the water, occasionally slowing down to wade around a bad place. When she stopped at last, he turned the glasses on her. They brought her very close and clear despite the screen on the window and the intervening leaves. He saw her pause to catch her breath and then wade out into the cove—gingerly because of the muddy bottom here—and begin to swim around the reeds that grew out to a point near the dock.

She was being careful now, doing most of it under water and breaking the surface gently when she rose; then she was under the dock and he could no longer see her. There was not much doubt in his mind as to her destination now, and he held the binoculars steady on the cockpit of the power cruiser lying at the end of the pier; she would have to come over the stern since the bow was too high to reach from the water. When she came into sight she was moving fast, lunging for the rail and heaving herself up and inboard in a flash, so that if he had not been watching for her there he might well have missed her entirely. She did not appear again. He did not expect her to; she would keep her head down until she had wormed her way into the cabin.

Young let the binoculars down to hang by their strap about his neck. He hesitated a moment, although there was clearly no decision to be made; his next move was obvious. He had to go down there and see what the hell the kid was up to. He pulled the glasses off, laid them on the dining table and walked deliberately out of the house, pausing at the edge of the lawn to look back as it occurred to him that he had never seen the place from the outside to remember it, having been in pretty poor shape the day he was brought here. It was an old brick house, he saw now, with white trim that needed painting. The lines were square and formal and heavy; it was a house that took itself seriously, but the shaggy condition of the grounds gave it an unkempt look, like that of an elderly aristocratic gentleman with alcoholic tendencies. It was a house that had seen better days, and nicer people.

Young swung himself about, knowing that he was stalling, and looked down the path at the dock below, and thought, sourly, *It's only a little girl, junior, a hundred and ten pounds on the hoof, if that; and you've got a gun.* There was another thought that was trying to claim his attention; but he gave it no chance. He drew a deep breath that hurt the bruises and torn ligaments of his chest but did not seem to touch the emptiness in his lungs, and started down.

The steeper portions of the path were laid in shallow stone steps around which the rains had cut treacherous gullies; and nobody had cut the brush back all spring. Young made the awkward descent with care, since his knees were still not entirely dependable. It was not his intention to hide his approach—he had no strength to spare for that—and he made no attempt at silence; when he reached the dock at last his steps resounded hollowly on the heavy boards. The dock was longer than it had seemed from above. The *Amberjack* lay uneasy at the extreme end of it, stirred by the waves rolling in from the estuary, with a constant creaking of dock-lines and fenders. As Young had told Elizabeth, it was a poor place to keep a boat tied up permanently. The deckhouse windows were shielded by blinds on the inside, so that there was no seeing who was aboard.

Young visualized the probable plan of the boat as he moved forward. On a forty-footer there would not be much variation from the standard pattern: an open cockpit at the stern, the glassed-in deckhouse with steering wheel and engine controls, and, down a short companionway, the galley, head, and sleeping quarters under the forward deck. As Young came closer he noted that the forward hatch was open for ventilation; and the thought that he preferred not to consider stirred again at the back of his mind. He was aware of the old, familiar, low-tide smells; he noticed that the tide was still ebbing, although, by the looks of it, they did not have much tide this far up the Bay. He remembered places he had known where a ten-foot rise and fall was nothing out of the ordinary; it seemed to him that he had been away from salt water for a long time.

He paused at the end of the dock, took a grip of the gun in his trousers pocket, and waited for the boat to swing back in to him. Then he stepped down into the cockpit that was still, he noticed, splashed wetly where the kid had hauled herself aboard. He took a step forward. The deckhouse doors were open so that he could see inside, and she was sitting on the port settee, just abaft the helmsman's seat. She had her foot in her lap, and a first-aid kit was open on the leather cushion beside her. She looked up without surprise as he stepped inside.

"Hi, Larry," she said.

Chapter Thirteen

Bonita Decker laughed. "Toss me a hanky, will you, Larry? I'm bleeding all over the lousy boat.... Thanks. Now peel me one of those Band-Aids. God damn people who heave bottles and stuff in the water, anyway!"

Young found himself helping her mechanically, although this involved taking his hand from the gun in his pocket. He was uneasily aware of the strained and limited motion of the boat against the dock; he had not had a deck under his feet for more than six years and the familiar heave and roll—the occasional jerk as the cruiser was brought up sharp by the fenders or mooring lines—brought back memories that he would have preferred to leave forgotten. He was also acutely conscious of the open companionway at the forward end of the deckhouse; and he admitted to himself now that he had been terribly afraid that he would not find the girl alone, and that he was still by no means certain that she was alone.

At some time during the past half hour it had occurred to him suddenly that a bold and ingenious man—a man like Larry Wilson—might well consider it both clever and amusing to choose for a hiding place a comfortable cabin cruiser tied up directly below the window of a wife who believed that she had killed him....

Nothing moved in the forward part of the boat, at least not with enough noise to be heard above the creakings and splashings normal to a vessel lying in this exposed position. Young stood by in silence while the girl covered the cut on the ball of her right foot. She looked up, holding out the stained handkerchief. He took it, trying to read in her small, freckled face—as sunburned as a person of her fair coloring could get—whether she really believed him to be Wilson or was just stringing him along. After all, the kid had not gone to all this trouble just to pay a surreptitious visit to a boat she had doubtless seen several hundred times before; she had come here to find something—or somebody.

Whatever the situation, it was clearly time for him to speak; he could not remain dumb forever. But when he reached for words he discovered that the days that had passed had erased from his mind all memory of Wilson's normal voice and manner; there was no picture of the man left for him to imitate. All he could think of was a whisper in the night and an armed figure running.

He cleared his throat. "All squared away?" he

asked. "Well, I'll take this rag below and wash it out."

The nautical phrases sounded phony to his ears, but the girl seemed undisturbed. She closed the first-aid kit and gave it to him.

"Might as well stow this away, too, while you're at it."

He could not tell whether it was a test or not; obviously the little box was kept in a place aboard—presumably below—well known both to her and to Larry Wilson, and just as obviously he had no idea what place this might be. The fact that she made no move to accompany him seemed to indicate that she had no idea of the problem with which she had confronted him.

The companionway ladder was short; four steps brought him down to the level of the galley. He had his hand on the gun now, but aside from the constant motion of the boat itself, nothing moved. The galley was to starboard; opposite was the kind of dinette that could be converted into a berth at night. The area had an efficient and compact look of space well utilized; it was lighted by an oval port on each side as well as by the open companionway. Young found the headroom somewhat scanty for his height; although there was clearance enough, he found himself crouching a little to make quite sure that he would not crack his bandaged head against the deck beams. The problem of the first-aid kit solved itself when he saw, mounted on a nearby bulkhead, a white-painted cabinet the door of which, hanging open, was marked with a large red cross. He pushed the kit inside and secured the door. He dropped the blood-stained handkerchief on the drainboard of the stainless steel sink, took the gun out of his pocket, and moved cautiously to inspect the three closed mahogany doors in front of him.

The one to starboard opened under his hand to show him the head, with its manually operated, sea-going plumbing that, he recalled, most landlubbers seemed to find fully as confusing as the rigging of a square-rigged ship. The door to port, narrower, revealed a locker devoted to the storage of oilskins and life-preservers. That left only the full-sized door leading forward. He pushed it open and found himself in a neat double stateroom, quite empty, with comfortable berths on either hand, an open and empty clothes-locker, and a well-varnished mahogany dresser with a mirror above.

The stateroom, well forward in the boat, necessarily tapered toward the bow so that the two berths almost met at the forward end of the compartment, leaving only space enough for a narrow door, which stood open, held that way by a brass hook and eye. Young moved forward slowly and looked into the space beyond. There was a pipe-berth here, but this wedge-shaped compartment in the bow was apparently used mainly as a store-room and rope locker. It was lighted only by the open hatch overhead, which gave sufficient illumination to show that there was no one inside.

As Young paused there a moment, a rumbling went through the whole boat. He found himself gripping the door jamb tightly; it seemed to him that suddenly he could smell gasoline and fire, while at the same time all his senses were prepared for the first ugly lurch and rush of water and the increasingly heavy and sodden motion as the craft settled swiftly, carrying him, trapped in this tiny space, down. He cast a panicky look at the hatch overhead. An iron ladder bolted to the bulkhead made it possible to reach the deck this way. His foot was on the first rung when the starter, grinding away, finally managed to kick the reluctant engine into life.

He leaned against the ladder weakly. Presently he looked down and saw that he had dropped the gun. He picked it up and put it in his pocket. Even now, knowing where it came from, the sound and vibration gave him a trapped feeling; and he walked quickly back through the boat and looked up the companionway at the girl sitting at the controls.

"What the hell," he asked, "do you think you're doing?"

She cut the switch and the motor stopped. "Why, I was just seeing if she'd still turn over after lying here all spring."

He said, "Well, you scared hell out of me."

"Then you scare awful easy these days," she said. "What the devil are you doing down there, anyway, Larry? I shouldn't stick around too long, you know."

He said, "I was just checking to see what kind of shape she's in. I'll be right up."

"I don't suppose you've got a beer on ice."

"No," he said, "I don't suppose so."

He turned back and let some water into the sink and rinsed out the handkerchief. When he came into the deckhouse, Bonita Decker was kneeling on the starboard settee, looking shoreward past one of the drawn blinds that she had pulled aside.

"What are you looking at?" Young asked.

"Just checking," she said without turning her head. "Where is she?"

"Elizabeth? She's asleep. She went hysterical on me this morning. I had to call Henshaw out to calm her down. He gave her something. She's good for a couple of hours yet."

Bonita Decker hesitated, started to ask a question and checked herself; then she stood up and turned to face him and he realized with some surprise that she was almost a very good-looking little girl. She did not quite make it; she had a year or two to go yet. Somebody would have to knock the brashness and the shrillness and the profanity out of her, and teach her how to put on lipstick and fix her hair and what to do about the freckles, and how to sit and stand and walk—apparently her family had long since given up trying to make a lady of her, and you could see why. Resistance to discipline would be her strong point. She had a look he recognized; kids who were turned loose to grow up around the water developed an air of independence and self-confidence that was unmistakable, if they didn't drown first. It occurred to him that he might have had something of the same look himself, once.

But the stuff was there, Young thought; even now with the short red hair damp and spiky about her head, with her nose and shoulders freckled and peeling—with that skin she would peel all summer—even now in the green satin bathing suit that was in some way too scanty and careless to be really sexy, she had something to make a thoughtful man pause to look at her twice. It was all the more interesting because she had clearly not discovered it herself; or if she had, it had scared her, and she had decided to pay no attention to it. She was getting along fine being a kid and did not want to change. But the change would come, Young thought, and not too long from now—she was old enough—and she was going to play hell with a lot of men until she found one big enough and tough enough to beat her ears down. It would take quite a man.

Looking at her, Young had forgotten, for a moment,

the circumstances that had brought them together here; then he remembered Lawrence Wilson. Doubtless Wilson had seen the promise he, Young, was seeing now, and had elected himself to teach the kid the facts of life—which meant, in turn, that she could hardly be as unawakened as she looked, not after playing around with a man like Wilson for a whole summer. She was a phony like the rest of them, Young reflected grimly, and that tough-but-innocent-little-kid pose was nothing but an attitude she found useful. It was like Elizabeth's wistful hopelessness, or Henshaw's bitter futility, or Wilson's hearty good-fellowship; it was like his own attitude of rueful self-contempt. It was a mask behind which, like the rest of them, she hid from others—and perhaps even from herself—her real fears and desires, her pretty little schemes and cheap ambitions.

"Larry," she said. "What's the matter, Larry? You're looking at me so—"

"How can you tell how I'm looking?" Young said. "With these damn bandages?" It occurred to him that he had said the same thing before; and Bonita Decker's reaction was very similar to what Elizabeth's had been.

"Bandages!" the red-haired girl breathed. "Oh, Larry, bandages! Do you think I can't—?" She checked herself and took a step forward. "Larry, is anything the matter? Is something wrong? Are you scared I won't— Are you going to have a big scar or something? Is that why you've been acting so strange? Do you really think it would make any— *This* is how much I care about that!" she cried, and took another step forward and, rising on tiptoe, threw her arms about his neck. "Oh, Larry, Larry—!"

For a moment he was holding her small, hard body, still wet from the river, against him. Her arms were tight about his neck, and her face was close, and her lips, that he had once thought thin and reckless, looked soft and willing enough now. It seemed an easy enough thing to do—even a pleasant one—but suddenly he could not do it. You could carry a masquerade only so far. You might feel quite justified in stepping into the shoes of a man who had tried to kill you; you could without qualms take over his home and eat his food. You could even plan to run away with the wife who detested him. But you could not, in his name, accept the mistaken kisses of a girl who loved him.

He took her by the shoulders and pushed her away. "Take it easy, Red," he said. "Relax, take a deep breath, and start over again."

Her face seemed to crumple. "But Larry—"

"Ah hell" he said. "I'm not Larry, Miss Decker. Now sit down somewhere and behave yourself, damn it. You're getting me all wet."

Chapter Fourteen

She took two steps backward, staring up at him. Her incredulous scrutiny made him impatient. "I am not Larry Wilson," he said, repeating himself more distinctly for her benefit. "Catch on, Red? I never was Larry Wilson and I never will be, and just between you and me, it's one of the few things I have left to be proud and thankful for. Come the last Thursday in November this year, and no matter how rough things are for me—and I expect they'll be plenty rough—I'll be able to cheer myself with the thought that they aren't quite as bad as they might be. I may be a louse and a bum and a few other things, but at least I'm not Larry Wilson. It will be something to give thanks for—"

He checked himself abruptly, because the girl facing him had laughed. It was his turn to stare, uneasily, with the thought that he had already coped with one bout of hysterics that morning; but Bonita Decker's laughter was healthy enough, and she controlled it easily.

"I'm sorry," she gasped, "but I couldn't help...."

Damn it, sailor, do you know you've just cost me five bucks?"

He frowned. "Five—"

"Yes," she said. "I had a bet on with Aunt Molly Parr. She said the way to make you speak up was for me to make love to you. She said no decent young man would let a girl kiss him under false pretenses. I wanted to know what the hell made her think you were a decent young man. We put five bucks on it."

Then her smile faded, and they faced each other warily. Presently the boat brought up against the dock fenders with a jolt; the girl took the shock with her knees but Young, weak and tired, had to reach out a hand to steady himself. He saw the faint crouching movement she made at his gesture before she realized it was not aimed at her; and he understood the strain the kid must be under, facing, in these cramped quarters, a man twice her size whose face and expression were hidden from her so that she could have no real warning of what his intentions might be.

He asked, "How long have you known?"

"That you weren't Larry? Why," she said, "I knew something was screwy the minute I saw you two days ago; hell, I've known Larry all my life. I don't pretend I caught on right away; I mean, when you go visiting a sick friend you hardly expect to find a complete stranger in the bed, but after I'd got thinking about it—"

"Carry on," he said as she paused.

"Well, Larry's pretty big but he doesn't *look* big, if you know what I mean. He's—well, he's a smooth kind of a man. When I started thinking of you in that damn bed— You're a hell of a big, hairy bruiser, you know, sailor. Of course, I haven't seen Larry for six months and in spite of what his wife thinks I'm not in the habit of seeing him in pajamas, but just the same—" She moved her bare, freckled shoulders briefly. "So I got Aunt Molly to take a look at you and she said while she didn't remember Larry any too clearly—he never visits Laurel Hill any more often than he has to—she was pretty well up on heredity, what with dogs and horses and things. She said that to the best of her knowledge none of the Wilsons had ever come through with a male with that kind of football shoulders since Cousin Loretta Mae Wilson ran off with a stevedore back in the nineties. Besides, you kept your hands hidden. Larry's always kind of proud of his hands and waves them around to show them off; he thinks they're aristocratic. And the hospital records didn't show anything wrong with the patient's hands—"

"Oh, you checked at the hospital?"

"You're damn right I checked at the hospital," she said. "I wanted to know what the hell was going on! Like I said, I didn't quite catch on at first; I only got to look at you for a moment, remember, and the light was wrong. What I first thought was that Larry had got a bad crack on the head—amnesia or something—and that *she* had taken advantage of it to get him where she could keep an eye on him. Of course, the hospital said you seemed perfectly normal, so that was out. It was driving back from Rogerstown that I got the idea you might not be Larry at all, and stopped off at Laurel Hill to get Aunt Molly to help me. She thought I was crazy at first, but she kind of likes crazy people, being a little eccentric herself."

Young could not help grinning briefly. "I know what you mean," he said, remembering the formidable old lady with her cane. He said, "Tell Mrs. Parr, when you see her, that I thank her for her good opinion of me."

The girl looked at him a little oddly. "You're a funny kind of a guy for the spot you're in, sailor."

"I could say the same about you," Young said. "In more ways than one. What the hell brought you here today, if you knew I wasn't Larry Wilson?"

She licked her lips and hesitated, watching him. "Why," she said, "I noticed that the chain was gone."

"The chain?"

"Why, yes," she said softly. "*Amberjack's* mooring chain. Larry used to keep her lying out a ways so she wouldn't be all the time beating up against the dock like this. I helped him pull the mooring last fall. Well, it was all lying there on shore all winter and spring:

the mushroom anchor, the buoy, and the chain. But this morning when I sailed past I noticed that—that the chain was missing, so I came back to look around." The little hesitation was the first sign of fear or uncertainty that she had given. Young noticed suddenly that she was poised on the balls of her feet, ignoring the bandaged cut, and that the muscles of her calves and thighs were quivering slightly with tension; the kid was ready to dive for the deckhouse door if he should move. "He's dead, isn't he?" she whispered. "He's dead and out there somewhere with the chain wrapped around him; and you're pretending to be him so nobody'll know! I thought—There was a possibility you might be working with him in some way, and I didn't want to interfere; but you hate him, too, don't you? You're all in it with *her*....No, don't come any closer!"

Young had not moved. He said, "You're making a mistake, Red."

She shook her head vigorously. "I doubt it, sailor," she said breathlessly. "I doubt it very much. First she ruined him and then she killed him; and do you want to know something? I'm going to get her for it. I'm going to get her for it no matter how many suckers she finds to take the rap for her—you or that old fool Henshaw or anybody else." The girl's face became sharp and her voice took on a shrill and ugly note. "I don't know how she roped you into this, but how do you like sharing her with Henshaw, sailor? Do you take alternate nights or do you just flip a coin?"

Young said, "That's enough of that, small stuff. Keep it clean."

She laughed sharply. "My God, I've shocked the man. I'm sorry, sailor, I didn't know it was true love!"

The strain was telling on her, turning her nasty, and he realized it and checked the impulse to retort in kind. Instead he said, "Shut up and listen to me. Your boyfriend is all right—"

"He's not my boyfriend, and I don't believe you!"

"God damn it, shut your trap and listen!" Young snapped. "I don't know what Wilson's up to, or what part you've got in his plans, but I'm just advising you not to go off half-cocked and run to the police with any story of murder. I don't think Wilson wants the cops any more than we do; and I don't think he'll thank you for—" He overrode her attempt to interrupt him. "Shut up! The man's alive, I tell you. I saw him last night. If you don't believe me, come up to the house and I'll show you the bullet in the wall where he took a shot at me."

Her reaction surprised him. She stared at him for a moment, then whirled abruptly, and there was a clanking sound as she hauled out from beneath the settee cushion a Stillson wrench that was fully two feet long and so heavy that she had to hold it in the manner of a baseball bat.

"Just stay where you are," she said. "I don't think you've got the guts to use that gun in your pocket, not in broad daylight." She started backing cautiously toward the deckhouse door.

Young said, "You and your boyfriend have a lot in common, Red. Did he teach you that little trick of keeping a club handy?"

She hesitated. "What are you driving at, sailor?"

"You read the hospital reports. Do you really think I got beat up like that just going off the road in a car? And guess who set the car afire before it started rolling. You look like you might be a pretty nice kid if you gave yourself a chance; are you sure you go along with everything your little playmate is doing?"

Bonita Decker frowned. "*Larry?*" she asked. "You want me to believe that *Larry* beat you up like that? With a club? And then shot at you last night. Why—why you're *crazy!*"

Young said, "Listen, Red—"

"And don't call me Red!" she screamed.

He made an impatient gesture. "Christ, what a lot of sensitive characters! Elizabeth blows up if I call her Liz, Henshaw has a fit if I call him Doc, and now you threaten to hemorrhage if I call you Red.... Talking about names, what's this 'sailor' routine, anyway?"

"Well," she demanded, "aren't you? You talk like one. And—" There was a small, triumphant smile on her lips as, holding the wrench against her body, she explored the brief green satin top of her bathing suit and came out with a small object that gleamed in the light as she tossed it up and caught it again: a single gold button. "How do you think I came to cut my foot, sailor? I caught a glimpse of this under the dock and sliced myself open poking around to find it again in the murk. A funny thing, sailor, it has soot on it. Now how do you suppose that happened?"

He heard her laugh; then she bent over quickly and he was forced to jump as the big wrench came sliding and rolling, clattering along the deckhouse floor. She was over the side before he had caught his balance again.

Chapter Fifteen

He stood in the *Amberjack's* cockpit for a minute or two, waiting for her to come up, but nothing broke the surface of the river anywhere close at hand, beneath the dock or the boat itself. She was, apparently, not quite sure that if she were to tempt him by swimming away openly he would not take a shot at her or perhaps try to run her down with the cruiser. It was not a pleasant thought, that someone should think him capable of cold-blooded murder. Yet, he reflected, you could hardly blame the kid for being careful, under the circumstances. From her point of view, she had taken enough chances for one day.

Young climbed to the dock and walked to shore, not looking back even when he heard, over the sound of the waves on the beach, a faint splashing that might, or might not, have been the sound of a large fish surfacing briefly. The climb up the bluff took a lot out of him; he was dizzy and breathless when he reached the top, but he did not stop to rest. Inside the house he went directly to the closet beneath the stairs where he had put the suitcases Elizabeth had packed the night before. He carried these into the front hall. Then he mounted the stairs heavily and entered the bathroom.

There was a pair of cuticle scissors in the cabinet over the lavatory. He took these, regarded his bandaged head for a moment in the mirror, and began to cut. The small scissors made hard work of the surgical gauze. When the stuff was loose, he hesitated for a moment, then pulled it away. It gave more easily than he had expected, falling down about his neck.

The shock was not as great as he had expected. The face that confronted him in the mirror was completely familiar. It was just his own face, looking badly beat-up and very bearded, but still the face to which he had become accustomed from childhood, with an island of tape protecting the nose. He drew a long breath, cut away the bandages hanging about his neck, and looked about for a razor.

When he came into Elizabeth's room a little later, she was still soundly asleep. He stood by the bed looking down at her; asleep she looked young and helpless but still desirable. He found her appearance pleasing and, in a way, restful, after Bonita Decker's brash self-confidence. The weaker a man was, he reflected wryly, the more important it was for him to feel that he might be able to be a tower of strength to somebody. No man was ever going to be a tower of strength to Bunny Decker.

Elizabeth stirred slightly. She was wearing no nightgown, and the movement let the covers fall back to reveal a bare shoulder and the curve of a breast; Young leaned down and replaced the covers, watching her with a kind of impatient tenderness as, disturbed by his action, she opened her eyes.

She stared at him for a moment, puzzled, then sat up very quickly.

"Careful," he said, grinning.

Absently she pulled the sheet about her, still looking up at him, wide-eyed.

"Well?" he said.

"Honey," she said. "Honey, I declare.... You look so different from what I expected!" She giggled abruptly. "Why, you're not bad-looking at all!"

"Thanks," he said dryly.

"I declare," she said, "I must have been expecting a Frankenstein or something.... David, you look swell, hear? Don't get mad just because I— Oh, honey, come here!" she said, holding out her arms to him, and he went to his knees beside the bed, and several moments passed breathlessly. Presently she drew away and tucked about her the sheet that had become displaced, and looked around, clearly remembering certain things. "Bob—"

"Henshaw left a couple of hours ago."

"Did—did he tell you what—"

"Uhuh. The reports of your husband's death were

greatly exaggerated. By him." As he said this, it occurred to Young that the woman in his arms was now a married woman again, with a husband very much alive. Somehow this did not seem to change the situation greatly. He said, "Congratulations on being a lousy shot, Mrs. Wilson."

She shook her head quickly. "Honey, don't. It—isn't funny."

He grimaced at this. "You seemed to find it hilarious," he pointed out. She did not smile. He said, a little annoyed, "Sorry, just kidding." He turned to the closet and searched through the jumble of clothes until he found a housecoat. It was quilted and too warm for the weather but he did not want to see her again in the soiled negligee that made her look like a tramp, which was the only other garment of the sort he could find. He threw the housecoat on the bed. "You've got time to take a shower, if you want to, but make it snappy," he said. "We're moving out of here." He looked down at her for a moment. "That is, if you still want to, now that you're no longer a murderess."

She asked, "Do you—still want me to, David?"

He said almost stiffly, "Of course. But it's hardly fair to you, now. There's no reason you should give up all this to trail along with a—with me."

"Give up what, honey? All I have here is a kitchen and some clothes."

"You may not have either where we'll have to go."

"I'll have you," she said, smiling.

"That," he said, "is an item of dubious value. I'm not much of a bargain to anybody, Elizabeth. In fact, certain people probably already figure me a total loss—"

She smiled. "Honey, that makes two of us. We'll both be total losses together, hear? Now get out of here so that I can get out of bed.... David?" Her last word checked him at the door.

"Yes?"

"David, is something wrong? Why did you take off the bandages? Did anything happen while I was asleep?"

He hesitated. "Yes." he said. "We had a visitor. With red hair. Elizabeth, what did you do with that uniform?"

"Uniform?"

"Yes," he said impatiently. "The uniform. My uniform, that you told me your husband was wearing when he came here. You said he was strutting around—"

"Why, what difference— We burned it, honey. In the fireplace. Bob thought it was better, because of the buttons."

"And what about the buttons? What happened to them?"

"Why, we picked them out of the ashes and Bob took them down to the dock and threw them into the river." She reached for the housecoat and started putting it on as she sat there. "Honey, why? And do you mean to tell me the Decker brat had the nerve to come here again? What did she want, and what did you—"

Young said, "Darling, it's a damn good thing you're no better shot than you are, because you certainly fouled up this operation, you and your medical accomplice. God, to pick a chain that was practically a local landmark to sink the body with! The kid spotted it missing and drew the obvious conclusion; I don't know whether I managed to talk her out of it or not. Probably she won't believe the guy's alive until she sees him; she's not what you'd call a trusting little soul. And those damn buttons— It seems that friend Henshaw just happened to drop one, darling, and our little red-haired pal found it under the dock. With soot on it! Like an engraved announcement that a uniform had been burned! She waved it triumphantly under my nose, and I don't blame her. Hell, the doctor might as well have handed her my name, rank, and serial number!"

Elizabeth was quite pale. "You mean— You mean, she knows?"

"Knows what?"

"That—that you aren't—"

"Oh, that," Young said dryly. "You underestimate the kid, Elizabeth. She's apparently known for days who I'm not. I just want to get the hell out of here before she checks with Washington or Norfolk and figures out who I am. There can't be too many Naval Officers missing around this area for her to figure out which one of them is me."

Elizabeth licked her lips and started to speak. Then, careless of modesty, she jumped out of bed instead.

"Honey," she said, "honey, the keys of the station wagon are on the telephone table. You get the bags into the car. I won't be a minute, hear?"

She was already dressing when he left the room. When he returned to the house from the garage she came running down the stairs, wearing the pink slacks and sweater of the night before. She stopped in front of him.

"Yes?"

"David," she said, "we're going to have a wonderful time, aren't we?" and suddenly she threw her arms about his neck and kissed him hard and urgently. Releasing him at last, she laughed softly at his appearance, brought a crumpled tissue from her pocket, and wiped the lipstick from his mouth, speaking somewhat breathlessly: "It's nice to be able to do that without worrying about smearing up those stupid bandages.... I declare, honey, I'm going to have to get used to you all over again." She turned him so that she could see his face in the daylight from the door, and touched it lightly with her fingertips. "Your poor face! It must have hurt just dreadfully, but it's healing up nicely, isn't it?"

He was impatient to be gone now, and he listened to her voice in a detached way, as he had responded to her kisses; he seemed to be standing at the head of the stairs watching the two of them. They made a peculiar pair: the big man badly beat up about the head and with a furtive and preoccupied look in his eyes, wearing slightly too-small clothes belonging to someone else; the slim girl breathless and uneasy, her hasty lipstick somewhat streaked now, in light slacks that were a little too tight in the obvious places, as was the thin sweater. The string of pearls was about her neck, and there was today a collection of metal bracelets about her wrist that clashed softly when she moved; it was too much jewelry to wear with slacks that were neither quite clean or particularly well pressed.

He said abruptly, "Let's get out of here, darling. We started leaving this place around two o'clock last night, and we're still here."

"David."

Her voice checked him again. "Yes?" he said impatiently.

"David, you love me, don't you? You wouldn't—"

"What?"

She caught his arm, looking up at him searchingly.

"Honey, if you should learn—something about me—"

Her voice trailed away. He studied her face, and suddenly found himself remembering all the things that she had done: the list that she had destroyed, her midnight expedition with a flashlight, her efforts to keep him from knowing about the boat that had entered the cove the previous night. He remembered also that when she thought she had killed her husband, she had not called the police, although the circumstances—if she had described them correctly—would certainly have justified her action in the eyes of the law. There had been no need for concealment—if she had told all the truth.

Looking down at her, he realized that there had to be some good reason why she was willing to leave this place which, with all its drawbacks, seemed to offer her a security that she was certainly not going to find with him. She was not a girl you would expect to share the fate of a nameless fugitive for love alone.

He took her by the shoulders and said, "You were mixed up in it, too? Whatever was going on here. Not only your husband, but you. That's why he knew he was safe in coming here that night?"

She hesitated, and licked her lips and, after a moment, nodded minutely. Her eyes had a furtive look that he did not like, as if even now she did not intend to be quite candid with him.

He asked, "Elizabeth, what the hell *has* been

going on around here? What is all this boat business, anyway?"

There was another brief hesitation. She looked away from him. "Why," she said, "why, honey, it's a kind of—of courier service, I think. Stuff from Washington, mainly.... Honey, I don't know!" she breathed. "I don't know anything about it. All I know is that—that I'd be given things to pass along, and there'd be signals, and I'd go down to the shore when one of the boats came in and give them— Or sometimes they gave me things."

"And Wilson passed the stuff along to Washington?"

After a moment she nodded reluctantly.

Young said, "And last night when you went down there—"

"I had to tell them to leave. I wanted to get them out of here quick, because of you."

"But they didn't leave right away," Young said. "Not even after I had my nightmare."

She glanced at him, and licked her lips, and looked away again. "I think," she said, and hesitated. "I think they had to meet—somebody. About something important that was expected—Honey, I don't *know!*" she cried. "What difference—"

"If you and your husband were accomplices," Young said, "Why did you shoot him, Elizabeth?"

She was silent for a moment, then she swung

about to look up at him directly. "Why, because I hated him, honey!" she cried. "Because I hated what he was making me do. Because I wanted to—to break away and he wouldn't let me! I told him I wasn't going to have any more to do with it; that's when he hit me and I grabbed the gun; that's how it really happened!"

Young said, "But if you really wanted to break away, why didn't you get in touch with the F.B.I. long ago and tell them what you knew?"

She said sharply, "And go through all that, and be marked as an ex-Communist for the rest of my life, as if I cared a hoot about their stupid politics? Honey, don't you believe me?" she demanded. "You should be able to understand. I declare, you're a fine one to criticize."

"I'm not criticizing, Elizabeth." He went on quickly: "Tell me, this boat last night. You haven't any idea at all what they were up to? Something important, you said."

She made a face. "Oh, they're always getting hold of something fantastically important, to hear them talk. Every time one of them manages to get anything at all, it's important and he starts screaming for a boat to take it off his hands, as if we could move those silly little put-puts around like checkers. What difference does it make, anyway?"

Young asked, "Did they get it, whatever it was? The people on the boat, that is."

"No, I think there was some hitch. They're going to try to make the contact again tonight, somewhere down the Bay; they decided it was safer than waiting around here with you screaming your head off."

"Do you know where they're meeting tonight?"

"Why, I reckon they'll use the usual emergency rendezvous near Elder Island.... Honey," she said quickly, "what are you driving at?"

Young hesitated. "We could—" he said. "We could make a phone call before we pulled out, couldn't we? I mean, damn it, Elizabeth, maybe it *is* something important—"

"Are you crazy?" she demanded. "Do you want to ruin everything, David? If you call from here—from anywhere—they'll trace it and we won't get twenty miles.... We've got to have time, honey. We've got to get rid of that station wagon and buy a little second-hand car of some kind. We've got to get away, maybe out of the country. We've got to got to get more money out of Larry's accounts, and how are we going to do that if anybody gets suspicious.... Honey, be sensible!" she cried. "I declare, this is no time for you to get an attack of patriotism."

"But—"

Her voice sharpened. "I declare, honey, anybody'd think you didn't want to go away with me! Anybody'd think you wanted to spend a term in Portsmouth for desertion instead. Do you think they'll appreciate your calling them up? Do you think they'll pin another medal on you and let us go? Don't be a fool, hear? They'll give you a court-martial and probably try you for being a spy as well, not to mention what they'll do to me; and some fathead in Washington will take the credit for breaking up the ring while we both go to jail." Her voice broke, and she swayed against him with a movement, clearly deliberate, that made him conscious of the shape of her breasts beneath the thin sweater. "Honey, don't throw our lives away for a silly notion!" she gasped. "We can have such a wonderful time together. I'll make it so you never regret it for a minute!" The bracelets on her wrist clashed softly as she put her arms about his neck.

He felt the frank promise of her body—and of her lips when she kissed him—and when he looked at her again he was aware, for the first time, of a real excitement and anticipation. The future might not be entirely black, after all. At least, he thought, it would be better than disgracing himself on shipboard in front of a lot of men who depended on him; and as for the situation here, there were people who were paid to take care of things like that. He had made a certain contribution in blood and courage once; they had no right to keep coming back for more. A man had only so much to give.

He freed himself from Elizabeth's arms, swung her around, and slapped her smartly where the pink slacks were tightest. "All right," he said, "all right, let's put the show on the road, damn it."

She laughed breathlessly, rubbed herself, hurried ahead of him toward the door, and stopped. She pried two keys from her pocket and threw them across the floor. "Front and back doors," she said. "If I never see this place again— You've got the car keys?"

"They're in the station wagon."

"I've got the money. Oh, David, honey, I declare it's like getting out of prison."

"Do you want me to slip the latch?" he asked prosaically.

"I don't care what you do. Let the place burn down, for all I care!"

He pressed the button, took hold of the knob, and started to pull the heavy door shut behind them; and he could not do it. This was the strangest thing that had happened to him yet. He was aware of the bright sunshine, and of the steady southeasterly breeze still blowing, and of the girl pausing to wait for him at the foot of the steps. He felt ridiculous and a little dizzy; and he was no more capable of shutting the door of the house irrevocably behind him than he would have been capable of putting the muzzle of the gun in his pocket into his mouth and pulling the trigger. The door had become a symbol of something; if he shut it he would have to go, and he knew suddenly that he was not going anywhere.

He glanced at Elizabeth, below him. The wind was fluttering her thin slacks about her legs. Her thick, dark hair, dividing itself, had blown forward along each side of her face when she turned to look back at him questioningly. She looked, in that moment, pretty and desirable beyond belief; she represented affection of sorts, and an escape from responsibility. She was, he knew, the one person in the world before whom he would ever be able to appear as himself. She knew him for what he was, as he knew her; and she would never demand anything of him that he could not perform. All other women he would meet would expect him to live up to certain arbitrary standards of courage and loyalty; and the trouble was, he would be fool enough to try.

He turned abruptly and walked into the house, moving directly to the telephone. More quickly than he could have hoped, he was connected with the Washington number for which he had asked. He spoke clearly and slowly to the man who answered, enunciating his words carefully so that he would not have to repeat himself.

"This is Lieutenant Young," he said. "Lieutenant David Young, United States Naval Reserve. I am calling from a place near Bayport, Maryland. I have certain information..."

As he spoke, he was aware of her in the doorway, listening. Presently she was gone, and he heard the sound of the station wagon starting up, backing out of the garage, and heading out the road at rapidly increasing speed.

Chapter Sixteen

He awoke, breathless, in total darkness, waiting for something, and it came: a dull, reverberating sound like the note of a cracked and muffled bell—the sound that had summoned him back to consciousness. He had a memory of stumbling upstairs after his conversation with Washington and falling on the bed with his clothes on. Reaction had apparently hit him hard enough to make him fall asleep instantly and sleep the whole afternoon away and, judging by the dim, striped rectangle of the window, most of the evening as well. It surprised him, after what had been said over the phone, that no one had come for him yet.

The bell-like sound came again. *Bell, hell,* he thought, and sat up, reaching for the gun under the pillow. With the weapon in his hand, he slipped off the bed, approached the window cautiously, and looked out between the slats of the blind. Tonight there was no moon, and at first he could make out nothing but the dim circle of the drive, the blackness of the trees, and the dull sheen of the river at the foot of the bluff. The lights in the cottages on the far bank had a dim and misty look. The fresh wind that had been blowing earlier had dwindled to a faint and erratic breeze. He could feel it cool on his face. After the days of having his head totally wrapped in bandages it was pleasant to have a face again.

Then a man stepped out of the border of bushes at the corner of the house and tiptoed out into the drive, bent to pick up some pellets of gravel, and straightened to toss them gently at the second-story window at that end of the house: the window of Elizabeth's room. They struck the screen with the dull, ringing noise that had awakened Young. The man waited, poised, with his arm half-raised; a large man wearing a light topcoat and a hat pulled down over his eyes as if he was afraid of being recognized, a man who was supposed to be dead....

Young gripped the pistol tightly, feeling a violent mixture of fear and hatred. He reached for the cord of the Venetian blind and shoved the gun forward.

"Wilson," he shouted.

His voice seemed to shatter the quiet, shockingly loud. He had forgotten that the cord was broken. In answer to his pull, one side of the blind rose part way; then the mechanism jammed. He jerked again, something gave way above, and he had to jump back, instinctively shielding his wounded head, as the whole blind came crashing down, with a tremendous, clattering noise. When silence returned, and Young, shaken, stepped back to the window in a gingerly fashion, no one was visible outside.

He grimaced at his own stupidity, and ran out of the room and down the stairs. He pulled the front door open, flattening himself against the wall as he did so. The darkness outside was silent except for the usual country noises; there was a shrill, persistent squeaking that might be due either to crickets or frogs, he did not know which. He checked the loading of the gun in his hand in the dim light and started out, then stopped. Suddenly the expedition seemed to have lost its point, and he could not help remembering that Lawrence Wilson undoubtedly knew every inch of the surrounding countryside by heart, having been brought up here. It seemed stupid for him, in his weakened condition, to go blundering after the man in the dark; and besides, Washington had ordered him to remain in the house until they got around to sending someone. The individual in Washington had made it clear that its agency appreciated being informed, but felt itself quite capable of handling the situation without the further assistance of members of the armed forces in doubtful standing. It was quite possible, Young reflected, that he would be making more trouble for himself in official quarters if he were to interfere now.

He put his gun away, swung around, and went into

the kitchen to get himself something to eat. The clock on the wall read nine-thirty, surprising him faintly; he had thought it was later.

With the lights on, the bright, neat, modern kitchen reminded him painfully of Elizabeth. *This is mine,* she had said with pride. None of the rest of it had ever belonged to her, not the big old house, nor the antique furniture; not even the expensive clothes in her wardrobe, none of which he had ever seen her wear except the once when she came to take him from the hospital. He could not remember how she had seemed to him then; later images had crowded that first impression, never very strong, out of his mind. He found that he was thinking of her very much in the way he might have thought of a girl who had contracted a disease from which she was not expected to recover.

Working somewhat grimly, he figured out the combination to the elaborate switchboard of the electric stove. He put coffee on, and broke a mess of eggs into a skillet; he had no fondness for kitchens or galleys, but a man who had learned to cook at the age of twelve on a coal-burning Shipmate in the cabin of a twenty-five foot catboat—such a man was not going to go hungry any time there was food available, even if he had managed to lose, over the years, that early enthusiasm for ships and the sea. The electric burners were slow in warming up; the eggs had just begun to sizzle when a car came down the drive fast and pulled up sharply in front of the house, skidding to a halt in the gravel. He could guess the identity of the visitors; that was the way you drove, he reflected wryly, when the government was paying for the tires.

Suddenly he felt cold and weak and afraid. He cut all the switches on the stove, not trusting it to behave itself unattended. Besides, he doubted that they would wait around for him to finish his meal, and it might be weeks before anybody came in here again. He tried not to wonder what sort of inquisition was in store for him, or what the Navy would think up when the civilians got through. He started out of the kitchen, stopped, and took the gun out of his pocket. Having that found on him seemed an unnecessary complication, and he dropped the weapon into a nearby drawer. Then he squared his shoulders and marched to the front door, switching on the lights as he went.

The door was still open, as he had left it. He was surprised to see no one on the steps. He moved forward to look at the light convertible parked below. The top was down and the car was empty. It was pale green, with considerable areas of chromium, and dark green leather upholstery. It seemed an unlikely vehicle to be engaged in official government business.

"Put your hands up, sailor," a voice said behind him.

He recognized the voice and turned around.

Bonita Decker was standing by the door to the living room, in which she had apparently hidden, upon his approach, after slipping silently into the house—a small, trim figure in light-blue denim shorts and a blue-and-white striped jersey. There was one of those long-billed white baseball caps on her red hair, giving her a tomboyish air, and a .22 automatic target pistol in her hand. The gun had a long and very slender barrel equipped with a high, adjustable front sight; and Young had no doubt, from the way she held it, that she knew precisely where it would shoot, to within an inch at twenty-five yards. The present range was about five feet.

She said, "So you've got a face, after all! Not that it's much of an improvement over the bandages." She made a little motion with the gun. "I said, put your hands up!"

Young looked at her for a moment, thoughtfully. The gun made him nervous; it was not only defiance that made him push his hands deliberately into his pockets, but the need to conceal a slight tremor that he did not wish the girl to see. She said fiercely, "If you think I'm kidding…!" He grinned at her, and forced himself to turn aside in a leisurely manner, walk past her, and back through the dining room away from her. In spite of his pose of indifference, he was thoroughly aware of her behind him—standing for a moment where he had left her and then coming after him. He pushed through the swinging door and let it close itself in her face. He walked straight across the kitchen to the stove and pressed the proper buttons in the instrument panel, causing a small warning light to come on inside the transparent plastic of each button, and the elements to crackle as they began to heat up again.

He did not look around, but he knew when she pushed the door open cautiously, looked around it, and shoved it back as far as it would go to make certain that no one was hiding behind it. She came into the kitchen with the long-barreled pistol ready. She did not speak at once.

At last she said, "You take some awful chances, sailor." He did not turn his head.

"Stop making like a movie, Red," he said, speaking for the first time. "Give your dialogue a rest. You're not going to shoot anybody unless they come at you with an ax, and we both know it. You didn't come here to shoot anybody; you came here for information. If you were in a position to back up any shooting with facts you wouldn't have come here at all; you'd have gone to the police or the F.B.I."

She said quickly, "I'll have all the facts I need as soon as I trace that—" She checked herself.

Young grinned. "Oh," he said, "so you haven't traced my uniform button yet? I'm ashamed of you; I thought you'd know all about me by this time."

She said, "They're so damn secretive in Washington!

Wouldn't you think one of Dad's old shipmates—But I'll find out, and when I do—"

Young said, "You're wasting your time in Washington, Red. Try Norfalk, Lieutenant David Martin Young, U.S.N.R., serial number 210934." He gave the congealing eggs in the skillet a poke with the spatula and turned to face her. "So now you know, what good does it do you?"

She hesitated, clearly somewhat disconcerted by his attitude. "It might do the Navy Department some good," she said. "Or the F.B.I.; they track down deserters, don't they?"

"What makes you think I'm a deserter? How do you know I'm not a member of Naval Intelligence on a special assignment?" He grinned at her startled expression. "I'm kidding you. But let's not start heaving big words around, Red. I'm just a poor damn Reserve officer a few days late in reporting for active duty; and that's not desertion according to my reading of the Navy Regulations. As for the F.B.I., if you've got anything to say to them, just stick around. They should be along sooner or later."

She frowned. "You've been in touch with the F.B.I.?"

"I called them around two o'clock this afternoon. The fact that they still haven't got around to picking me up seems to indicate that I'm not quite in the public enemy class yet."

"*If* you called them."

Young shrugged his shoulders and turned away from her to attend to his cooking. The girl behind him was silent for a long time.

"You had a gun this morning," she said at last. "Where is it?"

"Right beside you in the drawer," Young said, and heard her check on this. He lowered the heat under the coffee as it came to a boil. Bonita Decker spoke again.

"Where is *she?*"

"Elizabeth?"

"Who do you think I meant, Cleopatra?" Her voice sounded very young and sarcastic.

Young said, "Elizabeth took it on the lam, as we criminals say."

"Oh, so that's why the station wagon's gone. I noticed the garage was standing open."

"That's why."

"So she ran out on you, sailor."

"I had an invitation," Young said. "I decided not to accept."

"Isn't it a little late for you to develop a conscience? What kind of a deal did you make with the F.B.I.? Can they promise you immunity if you're an accessory to murder?"

Young asked, "What murder?"

"Larry—"

"If Larry Wilson's dead, that was a mighty substantial ghost I saw pitching gravel at Elizabeth's window about half an hour ago."

"You *saw* him?" she demanded. "Tonight?" Young shrugged briefly, letting his original statement stand; and the girl behind him was silent for a moment. When she spoke again, her voice was totally changed. She seemed to be speaking to herself, to be asking herself for reassurance. "But if he's all right—if he's all right, why doesn't he get in touch with me?"

Young glanced at her again. She was leaning against the counter on the far side of the kitchen. She had put away her own gun as well as the gun she had found in the drawer, tucking them both inside the snug waistband of her shorts. The brace of pistols gave her—with her slim, bare legs, bright hair, and rakish boy's cap—something of the air of a musical comedy pirate; but there was no corresponding gaiety in her small, freckled face. Young put the skillet off the hot burner and moved across the room to put two slices of bread in the toaster on the table in the breakfast nook.

He spoke quietly. "Why don't you wake up, Red?"

"What do you mean?"

"I mean," he said, "that I think you've been played for a sucker; and that's giving you the benefit of the doubt."

"Giving *me* the benefit—!" The small girl by the door straightened up angrily. "What the hell are you talking about, anyway?"

Young said, "When Larry Wilson needed a place to hide out, he went to his wife, not to you. Think it over, small fry."

"I don't believe it!"

"You don't believe that he came here? Then where did this hypothetical murder take place? Is it your theory that he was killed some place else and brought here just to use up a stray piece of mooring chain that was lying around? That chain's your only evidence of murder, Red; you'd better stick to it."

She flushed beneath the freckles. "Well, if Larry did come here, it wasn't to hide out. He had nothing to be ashamed of."

"The Navy Department seems to have thought different when they fired him."

"That doesn't mean anything, and you know it!" she said angrily. "If you know anything at all, you know why he was fired. He wasn't fired for anything *he'd* done; he was fired because they couldn't have a man in a sensitive position whose wife was mixed up in—"

"Oh," Young said. "I see! That's what he told you, that it was all Elizabeth's fault!"

"You're damn right it was all her fault!" Bonita Decker cried. "And if Larry hadn't been so damn soft-hearted; if he hadn't been looking for a way to protect the little tramp just because he happened to marry her in a weak moment—!"

Young waited for her to go on, but she did not, and he said, "I wouldn't say that Larry Wilson was a soft-hearted person, but then I'm prejudiced. Being beaten up with a tire-iron does that to me." He held up his hand quickly, as she started to protest. "Never mind, Red. I know you don't believe that, although it happens to be true. You don't believe anything you don't hear direct from our soft-hearted Mr. Wilson's gentlemanly lips, do you? The guy's a pretty convincing talker, I'll admit. I had a chat with him myself, and found him persuasive as hell. But let's take a look at a few facts. Wilson came here that night; you'll grant that much?"

"I—I suppose so," she said reluctantly, as if afraid that the admission was a tactical mistake.

"All right," Young said. "He came here. We won't specify the reason, since we can't agree on it. Let's just see what happened next. Wilson and Elizabeth had a disagreement. He got rough, and she grabbed a gun and put a bullet into him—"

"So she *did* shoot him!"

"That's right," Young said. "She did. But he came to in the boat on his way to a watery grave, all wrapped up in that chain you've been worrying about. He was kind of mad about the whole deal, I gather. He bullied Dr. Henshaw, who'd been drafted for the burial detail, into putting him ashore and keeping quiet about it. Henshaw says the bullet just laid our boy's scalp open for an inch or two and stunned him for a while; as far as I'm concerned, it couldn't have happened to a nicer fellow. He's still one scalp wound and a broken nose up on me.... Anyway, Henshaw was scared silly and did as he was told. He dumped the chain and kept his mouth shut, letting Elizabeth go on believing that she was a self-made widow. And now we come to the interesting part, Red. Here is our hero, wounded, dressed in some odds and ends of clothes that happened to be aboard the boat—they'd pulled my uniform off him and burned it, thinking he was dead....What's the matter?"

Bonita Decker said scornfully, "Am I supposed to be believing this fairy tale? What's Larry supposed to have been doing in your uniform?"

Young said, "Never mind that for the moment. Stay with this. The man's been shot; he hasn't much in the way of money or clothes, so what does he do? Does he go running to his little red-haired girlfriend who has lots of money and a nice cruising sailboat for him to hide aboard?" He looked at her. "Well, does he?"

She said, "You know I don't believe any of this."

Young said, "And I don't have to believe that you're innocently involved, either, Red. You've been doing an awful lot of snooping and an awful little bit of going to the police with what you've dug up. Don't get on your high horse with me; at least I've called the F.B.I. As far as I know, you haven't called anybody. There's only one thing in your favor, and that's the fact that apparently Larry Wilson hasn't got in touch with you at all since he's been back here; and of course I don't even know that's true."

The toast popped up, startling them both. He turned to take it out.

"And suppose it is true," the girl said defiantly, "what difference does it make?"

"Well," Young said, "I'd say it indicates that he knows you wouldn't have any part of what he's been doing, which is the only reason I'm talking to you like this, Red. Wake up, will you? Don't you realize the runaround you've been getting? He came to you with some sob story and got you to have that boat built, didn't he? And then the two of you spent a lot of time on it together? Everybody around here thought you were having a hot affair—even Elizabeth pretended that she thought you were lovers—but it wasn't anything like that, was it? You were just doing a favor for an old friend, weren't you; helping him out of a jam? You were giving him a hand in clearing his name.... I don't know why it is that every time they get the goods on one of those boys, there's always some idealistic sap ready to carry the ball for him."

He finally located the butter occupying a little compartment all its own in the big refrigerator. He kicked the door shut. "Wake up, kid!" he said without looking at her. "They were both in it together, Elizabeth and our boy, Larry. If they disagreed, it was only because she has a habit of losing her head in a pinch; maybe she was threatening to sell him out. Listen, I know that girl; she couldn't conduct an operation like this if her life depended on it. She's brittle; she cracks, when things get tough. When the Navy clamped down on Larry Wilson, he had to find somebody else to help him cover up and still give him an excuse for hanging around the water. You were elected." He looked at her standing there, and he saw that he had shaken her. But she was not convinced; she started to protest. He shook his head quickly. "Don't jump down my throat yet," he said. "Let's eat first."

Chapter Seventeen

He poured a second cup of coffee for each of them, watching the girl, across the small table of the breakfast nook, cleaning up her plate with a youthful appetite seemingly unaffected by disillusionment or heartbreak. Her suspicion of him did not, apparently, reach to the food he had cooked. Seeing the way things were going, he shoved two more slices of bread into the toaster.

"It looks," he said, "as if you hadn't eaten for a while."

She spoke without taking her attention from the business at hand. "I told you I spent the day in Washington; and when I drove past this place on the way home it was all dark.... I sneaked down the drive and saw that her car was gone. Well, I didn't feel like doing any poking around in the dark in a dress and high heels and without a gun; and when I got home everybody'd had dinner and the cook was still in the kitchen and she raises hell if I help myself and more hell if I ask her to fix something for me, and then Mother asks if I can't be a little more considerate about mealtimes and Mark shoves his big oar in—" She drew a long breath, swallowing. "Anyway, I figured I'd meet up with a hamburger or something sooner or later, so I just changed my clothes and came here. Your light was on, so I drove right up.... You scramble a mean egg, sailor. Is there any more of that toast?"

"Coming up," he said. "So you're a Navy junior, Red?"

"Yes, but I didn't know it showed."

He said, "You said something about seeing an old shipmate of your dad's in Washington. I suppose there's a lot of Navy people around here; after all, Annapolis is right down the Bay."

"That's right," she said. "Yes, Dad was Navy. Captain. Class of—"

Young grinned. "Don't waste that Academy routine on me, Red. U.S.N.R., remember?"

"Dad was killed in the war," she said, rather stiffly.

"Sorry," Young said; and after a moment he added deliberately, because he wanted more information about her, "He must have had plenty of insurance."

"What do you mean?"

"Your mother isn't buying you yachts and convertibles on a service pension, is she?"

"Mother married again," she said. "If it's any of your damn business. Mark's kind of a lemon, as far as I'm concerned, but the money's nice." There was silence between them for a while; then she moved her shoulders briefly, as if to dismiss her momentary annoyance at his prying, and leaned back comfortably in the seat facing him. "I could use a cigarette while that toast's making."

"Sorry," he said, patting his empty shirt pocket. "I haven't been smoking; my nose hasn't felt up to it. There's probably some of Elizabeth's around." He saw a pack on the kitchen counter and started to rise.

Bonita Decker said, "Never mind. I wouldn't smoke one of hers if I was on a desert island."

Young said, "Relax, Red. Save your adrenalin. Don't take it out on Philip Morris; he hasn't done anything to you." He brought her the pack and waited, standing over her with the matches; presently she shrugged irritably, took a cigarette, and let him light it for her. Then the toast popped up and she turned away to take care of that, while he sat down again.

"You're a funny guy," she said at last, glancing at him sideways. When he did not react to this, she said, "I thought you were crazy about her."

"Elizabeth? What makes you think I'm not?"

"The way you were talking about her a little while ago. Telling me she's brittle—"

Young said, surprised, "Well, she is, but what's that got to do with it?" He grinned quickly. "Lots of men like their women brittle and helpless, Red; something you might kind of keep in mind. It makes a man feel big, to have somebody depending on him."

She turned to regard him critically across the table.

"You're pretty big already, sailor. I shouldn't think you'd need a helpless female around to make you feel bigger." He colored slightly under her scrutiny. She said, very young and positive, "I know I could never love anybody I couldn't respect."

Young said, "People are good and bad. You can love the good and make allowances for the bad. What about you and Larry Wilson?"

She said, "There are only two things wrong with that argument: first, Larry isn't bad, and, second, I'm not in love with him."

"Then why are you sticking your neck out for him?"

"Because he's a good friend of mine," she said. "Of course, you're probably the virile type who can't understand a man and a girl being friends.... Because he's a good friend, and because he was swell to me once when I needed somebody very badly." After a moment, she went on: "Of course, I'll admit I was mad about him for a while when I was a kid—honest, I idolized the guy—but, well, it sort of does something to your faith in a man to see him make a complete jackass of himself over somebody you can tell with half an eye is going to be just a total loss to the community, if you know what I mean. I mean, it makes you kind of take a deep breath and wonder just what the hell he'd be seeing in you, if he should ever look at you the way he looked at her. Not that Larry ever did. I don't think he's yet caught on to the fact that I'm almost old enough to vote...."

Suddenly she was telling him all about Larry Wilson, asking him to understand Larry Wilson as she understood Larry Wilson. The picture that emerged from her description, of a gentle and kindly young man whose only flaws were a tendency to take himself and his family a little too seriously, and a habit of babying a boat through a squall instead of driving her as a real racing skipper should—not from lack of courage, the girl hastened to point out, but just from a love for boats—this picture was somewhat difficult for Young to reconcile with his own impression of Wilson as, even at best, a rather hearty and loud-mouthed type. He said as much.

Bonita Decker said, "Well, that's just what I mean. Larry's fundamentally a shy person, and he compensates in front of strangers by putting on an act like that. He never really learned how to get along with other boys, if you know what I mean. His mother kept him in Little Lord Fauntleroy suits till he was twelve. I don't know how he ever managed to get her to let her precious boy go out on the nasty water where he might get wet or even drown." She shook her head quickly. "I used to make fun of him myself, the way kids do; I mean, he's kind of a prissy person. You should see the way he keeps his boats; he'll have a fit when he sees the way the *Amberjack's* been let go this spring.... He called me up one day after Dad had been killed," she said with an abrupt change of tone. "I was hanging around the house wishing I was dead, too. I didn't even know he knew me from the other teenage kids around here; this was during the war, remember, and he was already out of college and working in Washington, commuting every day with a bunch of other men who couldn't find a place to live here. He said he was sailing a Comet in the Sunday races and needed a crew, and somebody'd told him I knew the difference between a square knot and a bowline.

"I knew what somebody'd told him, of course. They'd told him that the little Decker girl had been moping around like a sick cat ever since the news came about the Captain. It made me mad; I told him to stick to his work in Washington and stop trying to build up the morale on the home front, I was doing fine, thanks, without any help from him. He said he wasn't worrying about my morale, he was worrying about his boat, and did I want to help him sail it in the series or should he get somebody else? I went, and pretty soon he had me slaving over that damn little boat of his all week while he was in Washington, and Sundays we'd race. We trimmed the pants off them, too. Two years running."

She reached for her cigarette and found that it had burned down to a stub while she was eating and talking. She extinguished it and lit another, blowing the smoke out and waving it aside with her hand. She said, "Larry's like that, sailor; I don't care what you try to tell me about him. It bothers him to know that anybody's hurt or in trouble. It bothers me, too, sometimes, but I get over it easy. Larry has to do something about it, if he can: That's how *she* got him, of course. She gave him that poor-lonely-frightened-little-me line of hers, with a Georgia accent, and naturally nothing would do but that he marry her, just to cheer her up."

Young asked, "How do you know?"

She laughed at that. "How do I *know?* Listen, sailor, that was one romance I followed from a grandstand seat. Every Sunday, rain or shine, in the cockpit of that damn little Comet, I'd hear all about how he'd been making out with dear, sweet, helpless Elizabeth during the week. It was a rough summer, sailor. I got awful goddamn tired of playing Little Sister Bunny, I can tell you. I guess I stopped idolizing him then; he was such a sap about it. Hell, I'd never even seen the girl, but I could tell she was a tramp. If he'd just crawled into bed with her instead of making this big production of it—! God, it made me sick, the first time I saw them together after they were married. I mean, she looked just exactly the way I knew she'd look."

Young said, "What was wrong with her looks, besides the fact that you weren't going to like her however she looked?"

Bonita glanced at him, and moved a shoulder jerkily, "Oh, I suppose she's pretty enough, if you go for that damn sloppy Southern-belle type—all sweet and sexy—that can never seem to manage to promote two stockings without runs at the same time. I guess it wasn't her looks, actually, it was the way she acted, right off the Old Plantation, when you knew damn well they had to run her down with dogs at the age of fifteen to put shoes on her for the first time. I mean, if there's anything that gets me, it's that damn phony refinement. Well, we've got some elderly female characters around this neck of the woods—like Aunt Molly Parr—who can spot that kind of stuff a mile off. Phonies, they go after. A couple of them cornered her one night. You know: 'My dear, how sweet you look, any relation to the Virginia Sutters'—that was her maiden name, Elizabeth Sutter.

"I felt almost sorry for the girl; but, hell, all she had to do was look them in the eye and say that she'd never heard of the Virginia Sutters and that, if they were really interested, her dad ran a saloon down in

Temperance, Georgia. Or whatever he does down there. That would have shut them up. Who gives a damn about that family stuff these days? But no, the little sap had to try and play it smart; she says, all bright-eyed, why, yes, her old daddy'd told her they had kin up in Virginia....The old ladies set her up and lowered the boom on her. I mean, they had her so twisted up she didn't know what she was saying. She ran out of there, crying. The next party I saw her at, she'd left the Old Plantation at home, but she had a chip on her shoulder the size of a telephone pole; and she drank so much Larry had to pour her into the car and take her away....Socially, you might say she wasn't a howling success. Well, I felt kind of sorry for Larry, but after all, he'd asked for it, and maybe he liked her anyway. I knew enough to keep out of it; there was no future in having him weeping on my shoulder. But when he lost his job in Washington.... Well, I knew damn well he was no more a Red than Herbert Hoover, regardless of what people said. Since he wasn't defending himself, it was a cinch he was protecting somebody, and I knew who that had to be."

"I see," Young said. "So it was you who suggested to him that he was covering up for somebody."

"Well, hell," she said, "somebody had to do something for the guy; he wasn't doing anything for himself. I put it up to him. At first he wouldn't think of watching her—he said a man shouldn't spy on his own wife—but I kidded him into it by saying that we had to know just what she was doing and who she was working with in order to help her get out of their clutches. Stuff like that. I mean, he was still crazy about her, the sap; whatever she had done, he said, he was sure it wasn't her fault. The word he used was 'impressionable.' She was impressionable. Somebody was taking advantage of her.... If you'd heard him talk," Bonita Decker said, looking up, "if you'd heard him talk, sailor, you'd know he had nothing to do with it. I mean, the whole thing had him utterly baffled. All he wanted to do was protect her."

She looked at Young across the table with a question in her eyes, wanting him to be convinced now but knowing that he was not; the knowledge, clearly, frightened her a little. It was the first time in her life, Young reflected, that the kid had come up against the fact that a man shows a different face to every person he meets. She did not want even to admit the possibility that there might be another Larry Wilson than the nice boy who had asked her sailing to take her mind off her father's death a long time ago.

Young said, deliberately, "He was swell to me, too. He was driving clear out of his way to help me get to Norfolk on time. I woke up in the hospital, with these." He touched the taped places on his nose and scalp. He saw the disbelief and a vague, uneasy fear in the eyes of the girl facing him; and he leaned forward and said, "Red, you're betting on the wrong horse. I'm not standing up for Elizabeth; apparently she's mixed up in it too and it's a little late to worry about who pulled her in. But your boy Larry—"

"He's not my-boy-Larry," she said quickly. "He's just a guy I happen to like who's in trouble."

"Yes," Young said. "The question is, just how much of his trouble are you willing to buy." He drew a long, patient breath. "Listen, Red, this is the way I met Larry Wilson..." He told the story of that night, from the car stopping for him to his coming to consciousness in the hospital. Finished, he waited for her to speak; when she did not, he said, "That's your Larry Wilson, Red. Do you know why I have this?" He touched the tape over his nose. "I have this, I figure, because I broke the damn thing playing football once; and your boy Larry couldn't have a body turning up with his clothes and a dented nose, his own being nice and straight. The fire was going to take care of the other discrepancies, but he had to fix that nose, so he just gave the body an extra lick across the face before releasing the emergency and tossing a match in the gas he'd poured all over the car."

He stopped, as she slid out of the booth and got to her feet and turned to face him. "I don't believe it," she said stiffly. "I don't believe it. Larry wouldn't do a thing like that!"

Young said, "Well, damn it, I didn't hit myself over the head!"

"How do I know what you did?" she cried, suddenly angry. "All I really know about you is that I've got a button off a naval officer's uniform that might be yours, and that you've been playing footsie with *her*, and that Larry's missing. Why should I believe anything you tell me? For all I know Larry picked you up like you said, and you were thinking about deserting, so you slugged him and hid his body somewhere and went driving off with his car and clothes, only you smashed up on the way and wound up here."

"Where are you going?" he asked, as she swung about and started for the door.

"I'm going to call the police. I should have done it a long time ago."

"I couldn't agree more," Young said. "But the F.B.I.—"

"I'll believe you called them when I see them!" she said. She pushed through the swinging door and let it close behind her. After a moment, Young rose and followed her. He could hear her rapping impatiently at the instrument as he came through the dining room; when she saw him, she straightened up slowly, facing him. There was a strange, taut look on her face.

"What's the matter?" he asked.

She moved quite suddenly, pulling the long-barreled pistol from her waistband. She had to work at it a moment to get the high front sight clear; then she pointed it at him. "So you called the F.B.I.!" she said. "On a dead phone!"

Young frowned. "It wasn't dead this afternoon. Let me—"

"Stay where you are!"

He sighed. "We've been through all this before, Red."

"And don't call me Red!" she cried. She started backing toward the front door. He let her go, moving to the telephone as she moved away. He was aware of the slender gun barrel following him as he crossed the hall. The instrument was quite silent when he picked it up; there was no dial tone and no response when he pressed the bar and spun the dial. He replaced it in the cradle thoughtfully. Bonita Decker had reached the door now. He watched her reach back to push the screen aside, slip out, turn to run down the steps, and stop, still holding the screen door open, forgotten. He moved to her side. She was looking down the bluff at a yellow light burning in the cabin of the cruiser moored at the end of the pier. It had not been there earlier in the evening, of that Young was quite certain.

The girl turned to look at him, her suspicion and hostility suddenly forgotten. There was even a pleading note to her voice when she spoke. "Tell me—Tell me, did you *really* see Larry this evening?"

"Yes."

"Do you—think that could be him, down there?"

Young looked at the light, and the pattern of the evening began to make sense to him. *They'll use the emergency rendezvous near Elder Island,* Elizabeth had said, but she could have lied or been misled or, with the F.B.I. on the job, the plans could have been changed. This was why Larry Wilson's boat had been put into the water this spring even though Wilson himself had not been around to use it; for use in an emergency, if one should arise. *And the light, junior?* he asked himself caustically. *Don't forget about the light, and the character throwing stones at Elizabeth's window, standing right in front of the empty garage that should have told him he was wasting his time.*

But it had not been Elizabeth the stones had been intended to awaken; and it was not Elizabeth for whom the light was burning. If you wanted to move a man from one place to another—from a house to a boat, say—it could be best and most quietly done under the man's own power. Going into a house after a man who was known to be armed might be dangerous and noisy, but awakening him gently, stimulating his interest and his curiosity, leading him down the hill to investigate an unexplained light, after first cutting the telephone wires so that he could not summon help....*But why me?* he asked, but the answer to that was plain. He was the man who had sent the F.B.I. on a wild-goose chase after another boat down the Bay; if he were to disappear now, never to be heard of again, there would be no question in anybody's mind of his guilty involvement in whatever was going on; the responsibility for a great many questionable occurrences could be loaded onto his shoulders. They would not drag the Bay for him; he would be just another traitor who had disappeared behind the curtain.

"Yes," he heard himself say quietly, "I think that might very well be Larry, down there."

There was fear all around them. He wanted to run; but there was, he knew suddenly, no place to run to. It was almost a relief to know it; there was no decision to make. They would not let him get away. He could go to them, or they would come to him, one or the other.

He said, without looking at her, "Red, give me my gun, will you?" He held out his hand for it.

She shook her head quickly. "I'm keeping the guns, sailor. The way you feel about him, you'd shoot him without giving him a chance."

He wanted to tell her to get into her car and make a run for it, but he knew she would not go, and it would only lead to further argument. Besides, he was a little tired of sympathizing with people who bought chips in games too stiff for them, including himself.

"All right," he said, almost irritably. "Well, what the hell are you waiting for, Christmas?"

She said, "Will you give him a chance to talk, to explain—"

"You've got the guns," Young said. "He can explain all night."

They moved down the steps and across the gravel. At the edge of the lawn Young drew a deep breath that hurt the old bruises and torn ligaments in his chest but did not seem to touch the emptiness of his lungs. He remembered that he had gone down this hill once before today to see Larry Wilson. The girl beside him was looking at him; he wondered if she could sense his fear. He walked slowly down the path and she followed him. The night breeze felt colder as he neared the water.

Then they were walking along the dock, side by side. Nothing moved, anywhere, except the *Amberjack,* ahead of them, rolling lazily in the light swell from the southwest. The cruiser strained briefly at the dock-lines and then swung in to bear hard against the fenders for a moment, with the live, captive motion of any vessel made fast to a dock. There seemed to be no one aboard, but the light continued to shine yellowly through the drawn blinds of the deckhouse. Young stopped at the edge of the dock, hesitated, and stepped down into the cockpit. He turned to give the girl a hand, but she already had jumped down lightly beside him. She was apparently not used to being helped aboard boats, but the gun in her hand made her clumsy, so that he had to grab at her to keep her from falling. For a moment she was in his arms, a small, compact, surprisingly feminine body. As he set her on her feet again, he was conscious of feeling vaguely responsible for the kid.

The two men must have been crouching outboard, along the seaward side of the deckhouse, hidden from the shore. There was no chance to resist; one took Young from behind, and the other, coming over the cabin top, dropped almost on top of Bonita Decker, striking the gun from her hand and wrenching the other weapon from her belt before she could make a move to reach for it. No word was spoken. The taller of the two, armed, gestured with his revolver toward the deckhouse door, and Young stepped forward and pulled the door open.

There were two people inside. Elizabeth Wilson had apparently been seated on the settee to starboard, but she was on her feet when the door opened. He was not really surprised to see her, but her appearance shocked him deeply. The pink slacks she was still wearing were streaked and smeared with dirt, as was the light sweater, which was also stretched out of shape in a peculiar manner, hanging loose about her, as if, trying to flee, she had been seized by the garment and hauled back unceremoniously by someone who had no respect whatsoever for either her clothing or her person. Her face was soiled and bruised, and there was a curious stiffness in the way she moved, as if she were old or very tired.

"David!" she gasped. *"Oh, David, honey, I'm sorry, I couldn't help it!"*

He caught her as she came to him, but already his attention had gone beyond her to the man in the hat and the light topcoat standing by the controls at the forward end of the small cabin. He could not believe what he saw, even seeing the face thus, unmistakably recognizable in good light at close range.

Without letting the gun in his hand waver, the other took off his hat. It was almost as if he were removing a disguise; the action, as with most bald men, made him look years older.

"Welcome aboard, Lieutenant," Dr. Henshaw said.

Chapter Eighteen

Elizabeth was saying, "Honey, I couldn't help it! He made me tell him everything that had happened. He beat me and left me tied up for hours under some old house."

The doctor spoke a low command. One of the men behind Young closed the door to the cockpit; and suddenly it seemed very quiet in the deckhouse as Elizabeth's voice trailed away unheeded. There was only the distant murmur of traffic crossing the highway bridge a mile up the river, and the occasional creaking of a dock-line or a fender, and the splash of a wave against the boat's planking. The red-haired girl was the first to stir.

"But—I don't understand." She looked accusingly at Young. "You said you'd seen— Where's Larry?"

Young did not speak. He was still numbed by the shock of realizing the magnitude of the error he had made. He heard Dr. Henshaw laugh.

"Why, I'm Larry, Miss Decker," the doctor said cheerfully. He sounded quite proud of himself. "I'm the only Larry the Lieutenant has ever met. He made the natural mistake of taking for granted that the man who introduced himself as Larry Wilson—who was driving Wilson's car and had Wilson's belongings in his possession—must necessarily *be* Larry Wilson. And when a man offers you a lift on the highway you don't repay his kindness by staring at him, do you, Lieutenant? And modern dashboards don't give a great deal of light."

The red-haired girl looked from one to the other. "I'll be damned if I'll believe that!" she cried. "Why, he saw you in the hospital; you even came up to the house to treat him several times, didn't you? You can't tell me he didn't recognize—"

The doctor said, "Lieutenant Young's confusion is really quite understandable, Miss Decker. One night he is knocked over the head by a man he never really gets a good look at. This individual is firmly fixed in his mind as a dubious character named Wilson. Some days later, sick and in pain, he is introduced to a reputable physician named Henshaw, vouched for by the hospital authorities. Is it going to occur to him, in his weak and dazed condition, that these two men are one and the same person, particularly when all circumstances seem to indicate that the second man is twenty years older than the first?"

It was neat, Young had to admit to himself bitterly. It was just about like Henshaw said, except that Young had sensed something familiar about the man and his voice at the hospital and later at the Wilson home. If only he could have connected Henshaw with these vague thoughts at the time—but it was a little late for that now.

"But—but he claims Larry shot at him last night!" Bonita said. "He says he even saw him doing it! He says he saw him tonight, too!"

Henshaw said pompously, "Yes, that's really a very interesting psychological phenomenon, Miss Decker. You see, as long as I maintained, shall we say, my aura of respectability—as long as I was just an old bald fogy of a general practitioner being, er, made a sucker of by the wife of one of my patients—it never occurred to the Lieutenant to think of me in any other terms. Therefore, when he caught a glimpse of me on the lawn as an armed, threatening, conspiratorial figure dressed in the coat and hat—particularly the hat—that 'Larry Wilson' had worn that first night, he did not recognize me as the respectable Dr. Henshaw, but simply as the man who had tried once before to kill him.... Of course, this development was wholly unplanned. I was merely waiting outside the door to speak to Mrs. Wilson; and the Lieutenant's appearance caught me by surprise. Having inadvertently attracted his attention, I shot out the flashlight in the simple hope that he wouldn't recognize me at all. It never crossed my mind—I was surprised as anybody—almost as surprised as Mrs. Wilson, although I didn't take refuge in hysterics—to learn that our young friend thought he had seen Larry Wilson alive. Naturally I wasn't going to discourage the idea, and I prevailed upon Mrs. Wilson not to disillusion him. The Lieutenant's mistake worked out nicely for me; and tonight I put on the same coat and hat—my own, incidentally, reserved for occasions when I do not wish to appear as old, bald, hatless, sloppy Dr. Henshaw—in order to deliberately trade on his illusion that Larry Wilson was at the bottom of all his troubles."

Something about the choice of words seemed to strike the doctor as unfortunate; perhaps the idea of Larry Wilson being at the bottom of anything. He stopped talking.

Bonita Decker licked her lips. Her freckles were quite noticeable. "You say you were driving Larry's car that night. Then—where was Larry?"

"Why," Dr. Henshaw said, "he was where he has always been, since much earlier that evening, Miss Decker. He was out beyond the mouth of the channel, at the bottom of the Bay, wrapped in several fathoms of heavy chain, with a bullet through his head."

The girl looked at him for a moment without moving. Her lips were a little parted. Her tongue came out to moisten them again; otherwise there was no sign that she understood what she had just been told. Then she made a convulsive little movement as if to whirl and flee, but the two men behind her blocked the narrow doorway completely and she checked the impulse before it had more than barely suggested itself in action. Suddenly the tenseness seemed to flow out of her; she sank down on the starboard settee and, after a moment, drew an arm across her face in a childish, ashamed gesture to wipe away the tears that she could not control.

There were footsteps on the dock. The man in the cockpit stepped back to look and put his head back into the deckhouse to say, “Here they are, Doctor.”

A little excitement came into Henshaw’s eyes, but he merely nodded and said, “It’s about time. Keep an eye on these.”

He pushed his way out of the narrow, crowded cabin, and Young heard him climb to the dock, to be greeted by a man speaking in a low, guarded, yet somehow triumphant voice.

Young could not follow what was being said, and after a while he gave up trying. A little sniffing sound made him look at Bonita Decker, who glanced up at the same moment, defiantly, as if daring him to criticize, or even sympathize with, her grief. There was also a hint of contempt in the red-haired girl’s look; and he became aware that he was still holding Elizabeth Wilson, in an absent sort of way. It seemed odd that he should need to be reminded of this;

Elizabeth was not the sort of girl whose presence in your arms you would expect to overlook.

Yet she was meaningless here, he discovered. She was not a factor in the situation; she added no weight to either side of the balance, she was not to be counted on, by anybody. It disturbed him that she had been hurt and was now frightened; he was vaguely offended at the discovery that her sweater was gritty to the touch; it bothered him that its strained condition made it quite obvious to anyone that she was naked beneath it. He did not like other people to see her this way, looking dirty and terrified and a little indecent; yet the instinct to help and protect her was no longer a powerful emotion.

It was not a matter of resentment. He did not even have to forgive the way she had let him down and lied to him and concealed things from him—the way she had betrayed him to Henshaw and Henshaw to him—there was nothing to forgive. People were what they were, and he was in no position to criticize anyone else's weakness. She had never led him to expect a great measure of personal loyalty. Yet there was a kind of loyalty that everyone had a right to expect from everyone else who accepted the rights and privileges of a given society. He had almost betrayed that loyalty himself, so he still had no right to condemn her, but he knew now that he could not follow her across the line, not even to help her.

An unknown voice spoke with sudden clarity outside. "...no need to notify the *Marbeth*. Our people must be prepared for sacrifices, and she will make an excellent decoy; in fact, this is an improvement on the original plan. You should have no trouble in slipping down the Bay while they concentrate their attention on Elder Island. Proceed direct to the rendezvous, and scuttle the boat.... This is the last coup, but the biggest one. The reward will be great, at your destination, Doctor. I envy you. Don't forget to mention the others who made your success possible."

Henshaw's voice said smoothly, "To be able to make such a contribution is its own reward."

"Of course, Doctor."

"Naturally I will make certain that full credit is given to all." The *Amberjack* rolled slightly, accepting the doctor's weight. The two men in the doorway separated to admit him to the deckhouse. He spoke to them. "The courier will take you back to Washington." They nodded and moved away. The boat's motion told of their departure. Henshaw pointed the gun at Young. "Start her up, Lieutenant."

"What?"

Henshaw gestured toward the controls. "Start the motor. Take us out of here. Don't try any tricks; I'll be standing right behind you."

Something unpleasant happened inside Young at the thought of taking the wheel. He glanced at Elizabeth, who had seated herself to port; there was no help in her streaked and beaten face. He did not look at the other girl, not wanting her to see the fear in his eyes. He heard his own voice speaking with a kind of breathless protest: "But I don't remember— It's been years since I—"

Henshaw took a step forward. "I said, start it!"

Young drew a long breath, turned, and walked to the helmsman's seat. It was, after all, nothing; it was not like taking an airplane off the ground; nothing could happen to you in a boat. You could run her on a mudbank; that was about the worst that could happen....He tested the wheel under his hand, checked to see that the clutch was disengaged, and turned the ignition key. When he pressed the button, the engine started up beneath the deckhouse floor. The illuminated dials told him there was gas in the tanks, pressure in the oil system, and that the battery was charging. With the engine idling, the tachometer barely registered a reading; he shifted the throttle, watched the needle swing up into the hundreds, and brought it down again....A ship had more stuff and bigger stuff, he thought, but it was all part of the same thing, something he had been fleeing for over six years. He felt the forty-foot cruiser roll gently beneath him with that unmistakable, unforgettable motion that told you you no longer belonged to the land. The others must have thrown off the lines before they left.

"Ready forward?" Young asked softly.

Henshaw heard him. "Ready forward."

"Ready aft?"

"Ready aft. Take her away, Lieutenant. Starboard your helm as soon as you're clear."

It took him a moment to interpret the instructions; in the Navy the order would have been given as "left rudder." Then the clutch was engaged and the boat was moving forward and, as the stern cleared the dock, swinging obediently under his hand. He heard his own voice:

"Course?"

"Just follow the buoys out. Turn out the cabin lights—the second switch from the top. We'll dispense with the running lights tonight. You can take her up to sixteen hundred r.p.m. as soon as we hit the channel."

"Sixteen hundred."

"Steady as you go now."

"Steady, aye-aye."

He had almost forgotten where he was and who was with him. It did not matter for the moment that a gun was aimed at his back. He was doing something he had once done well and loved doing; and it was coming back to him as if he had never been away. He felt a quick sense of triumph; there had never been anything to be afraid of, he told himself; his fears had been as imaginary as the Lawrence Wilson by whom he had thought himself pursued and persecuted—a man already a week dead and buried! Then two things happened at once; as they came out beyond the shelter of the river mouth the boat rose abruptly to a cross swell, and at the same time the cold engine hesitated and coughed. The faint jar coupled with the very minor explosion seemed to take him back over the years to a night when he had felt a great ship pause, and watched the flight deck go up in a towering column of flame, before the blast swept him off his feet....

After a while he found himself in the cockpit being very sick in the cruiser's wake. He straightened up and wiped his mouth with his handkerchief. He felt weak and shaken, bitterly ashamed and cruelly defeated. Henshaw was standing, with his gun, in the deckhouse doorway, and Elizabeth was steering. The doctor gestured with the gun, and Young came back inside. He sat down heavily. Presently someone spoke beside him:

"Dramamine's supposed to cure it."

He did not look at Bonita Decker, but merely shook his head. Henshaw, leaning in the doorway, laughed.

"The Lieutenant isn't seasick. He's just frightened. He's allergic to boats, Miss Decker—a rather peculiar complaint for a Naval officer, don't you think?" The girl did not speak, and presently the doctor went on: "Suppose you take the wheel, Miss Decker. Mr. Young might have another attack, and Elizabeth seems to be steering us all over the Bay."

Chapter Nineteen

He could feel the steady vibration of the engine through his body; one of the deckhouse windows rattled softly and constantly behind him. The throbbing note of the exhaust mingled with the hissing rush of water past the boat's hull; he was aware of all these sounds, and he could feel himself tighten up painfully whenever there was a minute change in any one of them.

He thought bitterly that he ought to be grateful; circumstances had at least saved him from making a fool of himself on shipboard. The only thing to be done with a Naval officer in his condition, he reflected, was to take the poor guy out and shoot him; which, he suspected, was precisely what Henshaw had in mind. Somehow this idea did not terrify him. You could face these simple, straightforward fears; what the hell, there was nothing wrong in being scared of getting killed, as such. It was the complicated terrors that grow out of the kinks in your own mind, set off by things that bothered no one else, that made you feel like crawling into a hole and blowing your brains out. When you lost your lunch when an engine backfired slightly, or found yourself cringing at the smell of gasoline....

He saw the can, then. It had been placed handy, right inside the deckhouse door, a one-gallon can painted red so that even in the dim light no one could mistake its contents. There was not the slightest doubt in Young's mind why it had been brought aboard. *Proceed to the rendezvous and scuttle the boat,* the unknown man had said; and Henshaw had already showed that he was an individual who liked to sprinkle gasoline over things and watch them burn. Young found himself edging his way along the seat away from the door and the red-painted can that seemed to glow faintly in the darkness.

"David!"

Elizabeth was beside him, gripping his arm. He looked at her blankly.

"David, honey, what's he going to do to us?" she demanded.

"Ask him," Young said.

She glanced fearfully toward Henshaw and, after a moment, released Young's arm. "Bob," she said. "Bob, honey, you know I didn't mean— I declare, I told you everything you wanted to know. Why, if I hadn't done like I did— Why, the man said it was an improvement on the original plan. I wasn't really going to run away; I was going to come and tell you—"

Henshaw did not move. Young said, "Elizabeth, stop it."

She glanced at him quickly and buried her face in her hands. The boat ran on through the darkness steadily. The girl at the wheel did not look around. Her short red hair and the blue stripes of her jersey looked equally black in the meager illumination. Dr. Henshaw had seated himself on the settee to port, the gun on his knee; a big man, but bald and a little paunchy, wearing, under the gabardine topcoat, the worn brown suit with the sagging pockets that was his badge of frugal respectability. There was something rather terrifying about the sight of this unimportant man, a relative failure in his own world, who had managed viciously to change that world in such a way as to make himself, at least for tonight, important and powerful. It made you, Young thought, wonder fearfully how many others there were like this—not the dupes and the suckers, not the misguided, fanatic idealists, but the nasty little men and women indulging in secret treachery against the society in which they lived, in the hope of replacing it with one in which they would be a little bigger, one in which the people they envied would be a little smaller.

What's it to you, junior? You won't be there to see it, Young thought, and he could not help letting his glance touch, briefly, the red can inside the cabin door. The sight of it made his stomach knot up inside him with the knowledge of what was coming.

The doctor rose and moved forward to check the course over Bonita Decker's shoulder. The red-haired girl spoke, startling them all. Her voice sounded young and clear, only a little too strong, as if she had had to nerve herself to break the silence.

"Dr. Henshaw?"

"Yes, Miss Decker."

"Dr. Henshaw, what the hell is this all about?"

"Don't you know? You and Wilson spent a whole summer trying to find out." After a moment, the doctor went on, clearly pleased to explain: "Do you remember the Japanese sampans that operated in Pacific waters before the last war? Little ocean-going fishing craft that had a habit of casually turning up in the neighborhood of important naval maneuvers, commanded by surprisingly well-educated officers who always seemed to own expensive cameras? Well," Henshaw said, "it occurred to, er, certain people, of whom I was one, that the Japanese idea could be improved upon. Instead of a fishing boat of foreign registry, substitute a small, obviously American, pleasure craft complete with patent water-closet and suntan lotion. Oh, not the gold-plated luxury yacht with captain and stewards, but the kind of battered third- and fourth-hand little family cruiser or auxiliary that makes the Coast

Guard work overtime, the kind that's always running aground, or breaking down, or getting innocently lost in prohibited waters.

"Naturally, these boats had to be given places to file their reports, places where they could also pick up messages to be delivered, say, to passing freighters offshore. Such a station might be a boatyard where a workman had seen the light, or a dockside store, or perhaps even a cove on a pleasant waterfront estate where the maid or houseboy or gardener, or even the lady of the house, could be persuaded to develop the romantic habit of strolling along the beach at night. If the lady of the house was unhappy and dissatisfied and resentful because of certain unfulfilled social ambitions, it might not be difficult—"

Elizabeth Wilson stirred beside Young, but did not speak.

"—it might not be difficult," Henshaw said, "for a respectable, middle-aged professional man—an innocuous sort of person, really, and rather a failure in his profession—to suggest a way in which she might get back at all these people who had snubbed and humiliated her, by discovering a passion for night air on certain nights in the week. A little hard on expensive slippers, perhaps, but very soothing for the frustrated bitterness of a lonely young woman. And there was nothing to it, really. After all, the old goat was too crazy about her to let anything happen to her; and he really demanded very little, and could be put off with even less, with practically nothing, in fact, except a little co-operation with his silly messages."

The boat ran on through the night. Elizabeth Wilson did not lift her face from her hands. Henshaw cleared his throat and turned to look at the compass dial over the shoulder of the girl at the wheel.

"East southeast, Miss Decker," he said softly. "You seem to be working westward. I may not be a crackerjack yachtsman like you—I never had time to learn, my family lost all its money, you'll recall—but I'm quite aware that Harness Point Shoal is off to starboard. Let's stay clear of it, if you don't mind."

Without warning, he rapped the girl smartly above her ear with the barrel of the revolver. Young saw Bonita Decker sway dizzily from the blow, clinging to the wheel to keep from falling. The boat ran off course and straightened out again.

It wasn't as if the man were crazy, Young thought, any more than anybody who had ever suppressed a vicious or brutal impulse. The doctor had just left his suppressor at home tonight. He was just on a little jag of doing what he damn well pleased. Elizabeth's condition was evidence enough of what form his pleasure was apt to take; now it was the younger girl's turn.

There was pain in Bonita Decker's voice when she spoke again. "And Larry?" she gasped. "Why did Larry have to die?"

"Because he had a list of boats that you had helped him to accumulate, Miss Decker," the doctor said, rather maliciously. "Boats that had called in the cove during the previous summer. Of course, it's a popular spot among yachtsman—that was one of its advantages, in a way, although we also found it a little inconvenient at times—and of course we curtailed our operations here when it seemed, from her husband's being refused security clearance in Washington, that Mrs. Wilson had somehow come under suspicion. We knew, of course, that there was no reason for him to be mistrusted except for his connection with her. His subsequent activities—and yours, Miss Decker—confirmed our guess; naturally we did not overlook your childish maneuvers of last summer. We knew you were keeping the cove under observation."

"Then why—?"

"Why did we let our boats come through at all?" Henshaw supplied the question. "Why, because we wished to give everyone the impression that we were relatively unalarmed. To have entirely ceased operations here would have brought the authorities down immediately to make arrests. As long as they thought they could learn more about our activities and membership they let us continue to function in an unimportant way, feeling that they could pick us up whenever they wanted us. In this way, we could keep the apparatus intact for a single bold operation right under their noses: one final, important transmission"—Henshaw patted a bulk in his topcoat—"like that which is going through tonight."

"And what's that?" the girl asked skeptically. "A pocket-model atom bomb?"

Henshaw chuckled. "Even if I knew the details of what I am carrying," he said, "which I do not, I would hardly share them with you. But I am merely a courier. I can assure you, however, that a great many people will take the matter more seriously than you seem to."

Bonita Decker said, "Okay, it's important. What about Larry?"

There was a kind of strained impatience in her voice that caught Young's attention, a preoccupied note that said that she was not really interested in this conversation, that she was maintaining it only for purposes of her own. Young felt a faint touch of hope; apparently the kid had something in mind....Dr. Henshaw did not seem to notice that he did not have his audience's full attention.

"Larry?" he said. "Well, I confess that was an unfortunate mistake in judgment on my part. Certain considerations made me select, for tonight's mission, a boat called the *Marbeth*, which happened to be one of those on Wilson's list. I am afraid I did not take that list quite seriously enough. Since I was assuming, anyway, that we were all under official suspicion, it seemed unnecessary to take additional precautions against amateur interference. I did not, frankly, give Wilson credit for enough persistence; I thought, to be honest about it, that he must have given up his project. After all, he must have had over a hundred names to sift through, mostly of vessels belonging to quite innocent and patriotic yachtsmen. Yet somehow he managed to eliminate most of these, paring his list down to half a dozen or so. Not all of these were ours, and he had eliminated some that were, but unfortunately one of those that remained happened to be the *Marbeth;* and unfortunately it had been necessary for me to be in communication with the operator of the boat, making arrangements for tonight's mission." The doctor hesitated and cleared his throat. "Precisely what happened must remain a matter for conjecture. In a capitalist society, the concentration of wealth in the hands of private individuals gives them a certain power—"

Bonita Decker said, "In other words, one of your boys wasn't above taking a little money under the table."

"Perhaps," the doctor said. "In any case, the operator of the *Marbeth* and his assistant are paying their debt to the organization tonight....As for Wilson, he had learned what he wanted: the identity of the man who, in his opinion, was responsible for his troubles, myself. He not only had the information, he had proof, bought and paid for. If he had taken it to the proper quarters, our plans would have been wrecked, of course; but he chose to visit his wife first. He confronted her with the evidence. He said that he loved her and wanted to help her, and that they should go together and lay this information before the authorities. He wanted her to make a full confession, and said he would hire the best lawyers in the country to defend her....She is not a very level-headed young woman. She could only see the evidence, lying there on the table. In a panic, she conceived the idea of taking it from him and destroying it. She says that when she produced the gun, he laughed." Henshaw moved his shoulders briefly. "When I came there, at her summons, he was quite dead."

Elizabeth stirred. "I didn't mean—" she whispered. "I declare, I didn't mean—"

No one spoke for a while, and there was no sound but the steady sound of the boat's progress.

"No," Henshaw said at last, "I think we will grant you that, Elizabeth. You probably did not mean to kill him. But he was dead, nevertheless....We disposed of the body," he said in a different tone. "The bullet hole, of course, made it impossible to feign any kind of plausible accident; it was not likely that anyone would believe that, visiting the wife he had not seen for six months, in the middle of the night, he had immediately sat down to clean a gun. So we disposed of the body, and then we had to get rid of the car in such a way as to indicate, if possible, that Wilson had never been near the house that night. I drove the coupé and Elizabeth followed in the station wagon. It occurred to me that if I could establish Wilson's presence on the highway to Washington it would be evidence in our favor. I therefore stopped at a filling station and acted in such a way as to call attention to myself without really showing my face in the light. A few miles farther I came upon a Naval officer hitchhiking. I assumed he was on his way to Washington and decided he would make an excellent witness. I made a point, as Lieutenant Young will doubtless now recall, to make certain Larry Wilson would be remembered by the Lieutenant, and as a Communist suspect. At the time I wondered if I hadn't slightly overplayed my little deception, fearing that the Lieutenant would think it strange that a man should so bare his personal life to a stranger. And, of course, I spoke in the somewhat brash manner of Larry Wilson, although it seemed unlikely that I would ever see my companion again. I was disappointed to learn that he was joining his ship in Norfolk, with the probability that he would not be available as a witness.

Then I noticed that he was a big man, not too different in build and coloring from Larry Wilson. It occurred to me that it might still be possible to arrange an accident, with a body that carried no bullet wound—"

Bonita Decker said, "Only you muffed it." She laughed sharply. "It's a hell of a doctor that can't even kill a man properly!"

There was a desperate edge to her voice now, as if she were reaching the end of her resources. Young heard her gasp as the doctor, angered, brought the revolver barrel down across her shoulder. He saw her clutch at the bruised place and look around, and her eyes touched him briefly before finding Henshaw's face.

"Don't cripple your crew, Doc," she said. "You might have to steer the damn bucket yourself."

"Keep a civil tongue," Henshaw said. "And don't call me Doc.... Mind your course, now!"

"Okay, *Doc.*"

Young heard the interchange as if from a great distance, the brash, nagging voice of the girl stimulating the man to further anger; he heard the sound of another blow, the boat veered crazily, and he felt the sweat come out on the palms of his hands. It was clear now what she was doing, what she was waiting for. She had been holding Henshaw's attention, first feeding the man's vanity with questions, now pricking his arrogance with insults—she had been doing this deliberately, with one purpose in mind: she had been doing it to give him, Young, a chance to act.

The boat rushed on through the darkness, fast enough to pound a little against the light southeasterly chop; speed was a relative thing and twelve knots here could seem as fast as seventy miles per hour on a smooth highway. The voices forward had ceased; when Bonita Decker turned her head slightly to look to starboard, he saw a dark trickle of blood make its way down her cheek. She brushed at this, smearing it, glanced at the back of her hand, and rubbed it clean against her hip. She did not look around again. Henshaw stood over her, occasionally checking the course by the compass, occasionally crouching a little to confirm their position by a glance through the deckhouse windows. A lighted buoy swept past to port and was gone astern.

He did not know when the idea came to him; nor was he aware of having made the decision until his foot crept out to the can by the doorway and drew it gently toward him. It made a scraping sound that seemed to scream for attention but the doctor did not look around at once, and when he did so, it was with the same leisurely, checking-up movement he had used before. Young's mouth was dry, and his fingers were moist as he reached down into the darkness and found the cap, greasy and slippery to the touch. *You can't do it,* he told himself. *You can't do it. Don't be a damn fool; she'll blow sky-high when it hits the cylinders!* Then the doctor moved. It was too late for concealment, and he wrenched, and the cap came off in his hand.

Henshaw had turned and was plunging toward him. "What are you—?"

The sharp gasoline smell was in Young's nostrils, sickening him; he gave the can a convulsive kick away from him and heard the first burping gurgle as the liquid flooded out over the deckhouse floor. He heard himself shout something unintelligible to the girl at the wheel as he threw himself forward. She put the boat into a tight right turn that added to his momentum at the same time that it threw the doctor back against the settee to port. He landed on top of the older man hard, reaching for the gun.

Henshaw threw him off to the floor and kicked him in the chest. Young felt the pain blaze through him. For a moment he could not move, but he was aware of the doctor starting aft toward the can that had already half emptied itself. The cabin was full of the dizzying odor of gasoline. Young could feel it in his mouth and nose and eyes. He was conscious of the racket of the engine directly below him, and in his mind was a clear picture of at least six spark-plugs firing steadily while the volatile, explosive fuel dripped down through the cracks onto the hot cylinders.

The girl at the wheel cut the switch and the engine stopped. The sudden cessation of sound was like a blow; it was a moment before the lesser boat-and-water noises could make themelves heard. Young crawled to his feet clumsily.

"Red," he gasped. "Out the forward hatch, over the side, and start swimming. You can make shore from here?"

"Yes, but—"

"Tell them.... You know what to tell them. Damn it, get the lead out, sister! Pay no attention to that cap-gun. If he fires it, he'll blow himself to kingdom come with the rest of us, and that's no part of his plans." He felt a little drunk and rather dizzy. He put himself in Henshaw's way as the doctor came forward. "On your way, Red!" he said over his shoulder.

Behind him he heard the girl disappear into the forward part of the boat. Henshaw feinted with the gun barrel as if to strike at his head, then drove a left smartly into Young's ribs instead, knowing the weakness there. Young, trying to shield himself, tripped over Elizabeth's legs and was thrown aside; he grasped the older man's coat, and the gun came down across his wrist. There were footsteps forward, running, and a splash.

Henshaw stopped in the companionway, listening for a moment; then he turned and cocked the big revolver in his hand. His face was white and ugly in the dim light.

"Come here, Lieutenant. Start the motor. Head after her."

Young shook his head. "There's a gallon of gas in the bilge, Doc. One spark will set it off; and that goes for that gun of yours, too. We stay right here, unless you like to travel in little pieces."

He felt Elizabeth's hand on his arm and he glanced down at her and caught the strange fixed expression of her face. She was looking at Henshaw. He followed the direction of her look and saw the gun steadying for the shot; too late, he realized that the older man did not believe in the danger or, perhaps, was too angry to understand what he had been told. Young took a step backward toward the cabin door, drawing the girl with him; he felt her press his arm quickly with some message he did not understand. Then she threw herself forward and in front of him, and the gun discharged, and he thought he saw her body jerk with the impact of the bullet; but the muzzle-flame of the revolver seemed to grow and grow, with a swelling rush of sound that carried him back and up....

Chapter Twenty

The fire seemed to pursue him as he swam. The water came up to strangle him. He fought himself to the surface again. Even while he struggled to keep afloat there was a part of him constantly aware of the leaping flames behind him, waiting for the tanks to go....

A boat's bow almost ran him down and he had to go under again to keep from being knocked unconscious by a heavy life-ring thrown at him from above. A water-light went off in his face as he surfaced. He grasped at the ring and tried to keep the sputtering light—attached to it by a lanyard—away from him. The boat made another pass at him. It seemed as if all on board were doing their damndest to beat him to death with boathooks. There seemed to be something wrong with his arm, and when they twisted it, he fainted....

He came to consciousness again and saw the little redheaded girl standing by the pilot-house of the boat on the deck of which he was lying. She was wearing a sailor's pea-jacket that covered her from the neck to six inches above the knees and gave the impression of being her only garment. She was barefooted and wet, and she looked tired and irritable. Nobody seemed to be paying her much attention, although there were a number of men milling around on deck.

A voice above Young said, "Search him."

Fingers pulled at his wet clothes.

The same voice said, "As soon as possible, get the doctor to take that tape off him and make sure he hasn't got anything hidden there. They could have microfilmed it. Has the girl been searched?"

Somebody said it had hardly been necessary.

"Well, have a matron look her over again before she goes ashore." The speaker leaned over Young. He was a tall man in his thirties, in a light suit and city shoes that seemed out of place on this boat. "What did you say?" he asked.

"I said—" Young had thought he was speaking clearly, but his voice was barely audible. "I said, Henshaw had it on him. In his coat pocket."

The man said, "What? What did he have?"

"I don't know. He wouldn't tell us. It was a big secret."

The man seemed relieved. "You'd better not know, Lieutenant. If you have any ideas, just forget them."

"I'm fresh out of ideas," Young whispered. It seemed to him they were making a fuss over a lot of foolishness. There was nothing in the world small enough to be put into a man's pocket that was big enough to change the fate of nations or the destiny of the human race. Wars were not started unless they were ready to start; once started they were not won by secrets, but only by people and guts....

He heard himself whisper, "Did you find—anybody else?" She had been scared, he thought; she had been terrified, yet in the end she had saved his life, taking the bullet that was meant for him.

"Just you and Miss Decker," the tall man said.

Somebody said, "There's nobody alive on her now. There go the tanks."

Young saw a yellow light flare into the sky above him, and felt the breath of the concussion. He shivered a little. The tall man swore. "I don't mind its burning up. If they burned a few more copies, I'd be even happier. But how the hell am I going to be *sure*....Get that boat raised in the morning. See what you can find," he said to someone standing by. "Well, let's go home and clear up the mess. The hell with these nautical operations, anyway. Let's get back to dry land."

He walked down from the big gray house to the dock. The bluff here was not as steep as it had been at the Wilson place, but it was steep enough to remind him that he was again barely out of bed. It seemed to him a long time since he had been strong enough to walk down a flight of steps without having to be careful not to stumble; and it was awkward trying to maintain his balance with his right arm in a sling. The girl had brought her boat up the river. It was made fast alongside the dock and she was working in the cockpit. Her red hair was bright in the sun. She was barefooted and wearing only a halter and a pair of faded, paint-splashed jeans that were rolled above her knees. There was an ugly bruise on her right shoulder, fading now into a curious mixture of purple and green; an old bruise that clearly no longer bothered her. Everything that had happened seemed very long ago.

"Hello," he said.

She looked up, the varnish-brush poised in her hand. "Oh," she said, "you're up."

"Up again, down again," he said. "Up again."

"Uniform and everything," she said. "Gee, pipe the fruit salad."

"You can get anything at a hock shop these days," he said. He gestured toward the brush in her hand. "Carry on."

"I'll be through in a minute," she said. "Take those shoes off if you're coming aboard; don't mark up my decks."

"Yes, ma'am," he said. He worked his feet out of his shoes and stepped down to the shining deck of the little sloop to watch her. After a while he said, "I've been trying to tell Mrs. Parr how much I appreciate her having me here, but she's a hard person to talk to. Maybe you can put the idea across for me."

The girl said, "Put your own ideas across, sailor. Anyway, Aunt Molly likes doing things for people she likes, and she likes you. You're not supposed to thank her, stupid. Just send her a card some time when you happen to think of it. She gets kind of lonely, I think." After a while, she said, "So you're leaving?"

"That's right."

"Think you'll get there all right this time?"

He said, "You're kind of nosy, aren't you, Red?" She looked up at him quickly and grinned, and he said, "I don't think I'll get lost again. I'd damn well better not; I've got a reprimand coming as it is."

She said, "Well—" After a moment, she put the lid on the varnish can, straightened up, wiped her hand on her jeans, and held it out. He took it. She said, "Well, drop around some time when you're on leave, sailor."

He held her hand for a moment. Something in her attitude warned him that the invitation had not been a casual one. She had thought it over carefully before she gave it, deciding whether or not, in her opinion, he was worth seeing again.

He released her hand and said, as carefully as she had spoken, "Thanks. I might do that."

She started to say something else and checked herself; and he knew precisely how she felt. They had nothing to talk about now. The things that had happened were still too close and painful; they could not be discussed, and yet they could not be ignored. It was a good time for ending, and a poor time for beginning; they could do better later with no ghosts between them. He turned away.

As he stepped back up to the dock and bent over to put on his shoes, the sloop's auxiliary motor started up behind him. The sound startled him a little, but not very much; he finished tying the laces before straightening up to look around. The girl was watching him. He grinned and gave her a salute and walked away up the dock.